W0007444

Laela could see ahead of them the great house which had been built by the Marquis's ancestor in the reign of Queen Elizabeth.

The sunlight was reflected on a hundred windows.

A green lawn sloped down to the oval-shaped lake which lay below the house.

"Could anything be . . . more beautiful?" Laela asked. "To whom does it belong?"

"To me!" the Marquis said.

Laela laughed.

"Mama and I used to say exactly that whenever we saw something lovely. We might not own it, but we could hold its beauty within our hearts and so it was ours."

The Marquis did not say anything but drove on. . . .

*A Camfield Novel of Love
by Barbara Cartland*

Camfield Place,
Hatfield
Hertfordshire,
England

Dearest Reader,

Camfield Novels of Love mark a very exciting era of my books with Jove. They have already published nearly two hundred of my titles since they became my first publisher in America, and now all my original paperback romances in the future will be published exclusively by them.

As you already know, Camfield Place in Hertfordshire is my home, which originally existed in 1275, but was rebuilt in 1867 by the Grandfather of Beatrix Potter.

It was here in this lovely house, with the best view in the county, that she wrote *The Tale of Peter Rabbit*. Mr. McGregor's garden is exactly as she described it. The door in the wall that the fat little rabbit could not squeeze underneath and the goldfish pool where the white cat sat twitching its tail are still there.

I had Camfield Place blessed when I came here in 1950 and was so happy with my husband until he died, and now with my children and grandchildren, that I know the atmosphere is filled with love and we have all been very lucky.

It is easy here to write of love and I know you will enjoy the Camfield Novels of Love. Their plots are definitely exciting and the covers very romantic. They come to you, like all my books, with love.

Bless you,

CAMFIELD NOVELS OF LOVE

by Barbara Cartland

A NEW CAMFIELD NOVEL OF LOVE BY

BARBARA CARTLAND

Loved for Himself

J

JOVE BOOKS, NEW YORK

LOVED FOR HIMSELF

A Jove Book / published by arrangement with
the author

PRINTING HISTORY
Jove edition / September 1992

ISBN: 0-515-10932-0

Jove Books are published by The Berkley Publishing Group,
200 Madison Avenue, New York, New York 10016.
The name "JOVE" and the "J" logo
are trademarks belonging to Jove Publications, Inc.

PRINTED IN THE UNITED STATES OF AMERICA

10 9 8 7 6 5 4 3 2 1

Author's Note

THE hierarchy of the Servants' Hall continued in England up to the Second World War.

When I married, in 1927, my sister-in-law was twelve years older than my husband.

Her lady's-maid was furious that she had to give up her place on the right of the Butler for my lady's-maid.

There was a great deal of ill-feeling about it.

My Mother-in-law employed eighteen indoor servants, but in very large houses, the number were often as many as forty or fifty.

As one maid I talked to told me, it was great fun for the Under-Housemaids because they were able to dance with the footmen, who were chosen for their looks and their height. They had to be over six foot.

In the "Twenties," a young man of mine who was in the Navy and who was very rich had his own Puss Moth aeroplane. His Pilot, who looked after it, also valeted him.

My friend flew up to Scotland to stay at Dunrobin Castle with the Duke of Sutherland.

After the first night the Pilot said to his master:

"Did you have a good evening, Sir?"

My friend replied:

"Rather dull. Just a few people to dinner, and we played Bridge afterwards."

"Oh, Sir, you should have been downstairs with us," his Pilot replied. "We had a wonderful evening! Champagne to drink and we danced until one o'clock in the morning!"

At Woburn the Duke of Bedford at the beginning of the century every week paid two thousand indoor and outdoor staff.

As he said himself, it was a "State within a State" because with their Brick Layers, Stonemasons, Carpenters, Painters, private laundry, and other departments, they were practically self-sufficient.

chapter one

1818

THE Marquis of Mounteagle stepped out of his Phaeton and said to his Coachman:

"Come back in an hour."

"Very good, M'Lord."

The Marquis walked up the steps into White's Club and was greeted respectfully by the porter.

He saw through the open door of the Morning-Room that the man he was seeking was seated in one of the deep leather arm-chairs.

He was just about to go towards him when he heard somebody nearby say in a whisper that was quite audible:

"Look out, here is Mounteagle! For God's sake, do not let him look at the Betting Book!"

The Marquis stiffened involuntarily.

Then, with admirable self-control, he did not look in the direction from which the voice had come.

Instead, he deliberately spoke to one of the members on the other side of the room, whom he had seen recently at Newmarket.

"Did you come away a winner?" he asked.

"I do not have your luck!" was the answer.

Then the Marquis turned to the right and saw who had spoken in a whisper.

Without the flicker of an eye-lid he walked to where his friend Lord Charles Carrington was waiting for him.

"You are late, Johnnie!" the latter said. "I was beginning to think you had been trapped in the arms of some 'Fair Charmer'!"

"No, I was merely delayed by writing a note," the Marquis replied.

"Will you give me three guesses as to whom you were writing!" Lord Charles said.

"No," the Marquis replied, "and mind your own business!"

His friend laughed and, calling a Steward, ordered a bottle of champagne.

When the Steward returned with it, the Marquis said:

"Bring me the Betting Book."

"Very good, M'Lord."

The Betting Book at White's was legendary, having been started over a hundred years earlier.

It was greatly treasured by the members who, as they were all gamblers, added to it almost every day.

Now, as the Steward moved away to obey the Marquis's request, Lord Charles said:

"I think it would be better if you did not see the book."

The Marquis stared at him.

"What do you mean by that?"

"It might upset you, and 'what the eye does not see the heart does not grieve over'!"

2

"I do not know what you are talking about," the Marquis said sharply, "but I heard Perceval whisper as I came in through the door, 'For God's sake do not let him see the Betting Book!' What did he mean by that?"

"I know what he meant," Lord Charles replied, "and, as I have already said, do not look at the book when it is brought to you."

"I think you have gone crazy!" the Marquis retorted. "If it contains a bet that concerns me, then of course I have every intention of reading it, and if it is something slanderous, I shall knock Perceval's head off!"

Lord Charles sat back in his chair and sipped his champagne.

"I cannot think, Johnnie, why you worry over such a pip-squeak as Perceval!" he said. "Anyway, it is far more important for me to talk to you about horses."

He paused and then continued:

"I have just seen some at Tattersall's which would make a fine addition to your stables."

"I appreciate your concern," the Marquis said, "but I am curious about what is in the Betting Book."

Lord Charles made an eloquent gesture with one hand.

"All right, be it on your own head!" he said. "But I have always believed in 'letting sleeping dogs lie'!"

"You are full of quotations to-day," the Marquis said, "which means you are perturbed with what I shall find. I have known you ever since we were at Eton together, and when you start quoting, I know it is an ominous sign."

Lord Charles laughed rather ruefully.

Before he could reply, the Steward handed the

3

Betting Book to the Marquis.

As it was so old the leather was slightly crumpled, but written on it clearly in gold was

"WHITE'S—
THE BETTING BOOK
1713"

The Marquis opened it, turning over the pages of the early bets made in scrawling, almost illegible writing and came to the latest entries.

There was a number from previous years when he and Charles were fighting Napoleon.

For a moment his eye fell on a bet made in the year of Waterloo.

*"Captain Capel bets Mr. Brummell 5 gs
that Napoleon is not at the head of the
French Government in Paris within ten
days from this day.
    March 15th, 1815   George Brummell."*

Another bet made two days later and signed by two members read:

*"Sir G. Talbot bets Mr. W. Howard fifty
guineas to five that Bonaparte is not
at Vienna in three months.
    March 17th, 1815   W. Howard
                         G. Talbot."*

The Marquis turned over the page.

There were several entries concerning sport.

Then he read slowly:

*"Lord Perceval bets Mr. Hatton 50 gs.
that a certain Noble Marquis will not
be able to pick a flower until it is
known whether the Duke of D. will live
or die.
    29th April, 1818."*

The Marquis read the entry through twice before he said:

"If this means what I think it means, it is a damned insult, and I will call him out!"

"You will make a fool of yourself if you do!" Lord Charles said.

"Why? What do you mean?"

There was a pause before Lord Charles replied:

"Look here, Johnnie, you are my friend, and I have no wish to break up our friendship. All I am telling you—put the book on one side and pretend you have not seen it."

"Why should I do that?" the Marquis enquired angrily. "It is quite obvious that this refers to Fleur, and what the hell has the Duke of Dorset to do with her?"

Lord Charles pressed his lips together and said nothing.

"Oh, come on, Charles!" the Marquis said. "Whatever you tell me, I am not going to be angry with you. It is that little swine Perceval I dislike! He is just a gossip-monger, and if he has not got a nasty story to tell about somebody, he makes one up."

"Exactly! And that is what he has done now!" Lord Charles said.

Unfortunately, he spoke too quickly and the Marquis knew he was lying.

"Tell me the truth, Charles," he said.

5

Lord Charles sighed.

"Very well," he said, "but if you think I am going to fight you, you are mistaken. You have beaten me too often."

"Do not be a fool!" the Marquis said. "I am not fighting you, but Perceval."

"Very well," Lord Charles said, giving in. "What Perceval is taking a bet on is, unfortunately, the truth!"

The Marquis stared at his friend in sheer astonishment.

"Are you telling me," he said slowly as if he were thinking it out, "that Fleur is procrastinating in accepting my offer of marriage because if the Duke of Dorset dies and Settington becomes the Duke, she will accept him?"

"I always knew you were quick-brained," Lord Charles said.

"I do not believe it!" the Marquis exclaimed. "She loves me, she has told me so a hundred times, and is keeping our engagement secret only because her Grandmother is ill."

"Her Grandmother has been ill, to my knowledge, for the last three years!" Lord Charles said.

The Marquis drew in his breath.

"But Settington! You know what we have always thought about him!"

"A Duke is a Duke," Lord Charles murmured.

The Marquis finished his glass of champagne and poured himself another.

Then he said:

"What I want to know is—how was Perceval aware of all this in the first place? I have never mentioned a word of what I feel for Fleur and she for me to anybody—except you!"

"Well, I am not the culprit!" Lord Charles said hastily. "Then who is?"

"You will not like this, but Perceval's Valet is walking out with Fleur's lady's-maid."

"Do you mean the woman has told the man what is happening when her mistress has sworn her to secrecy?"

"My dear Johnnie, servants talk!" Lord Charles said. "In fact, nearly all the gossip that circulates around the *Beau Ton* comes from the Servants' Hall."

"It never crossed my mind!" the Marquis exclaimed.

"Of course it does," Lord Charles said. "Who do you think 'spilt the beans' over Henry's involvement with that avaricious little 'Cyprian' and nearly lost him the fortune his Uncle was leaving him?"

"It puzzled me at the time who had 'let the cat out of the bag'!" the Marquis said.

"Servants are servants, and as Perceval's Valet is a talker, I would not mind betting that practically every man in the room knows about you and Fleur by this time!"

For a moment the Marquis clenched his fists.

Then, with an effort, he deliberately forced himself to sit back at his ease.

He had been attracted by Fleur Munroe as he had never been attracted by any other unmarried girl.

He had sworn long ago that he had no intention of marrying until he was nearly forty.

He had then proceeded to enjoy himself with the sophisticated and alluring beauties who gathered round the Prince Regent.

They were all married and had husbands who were complacent, preferring the Country to the endless and exhausting search for pleasure which had swept London as soon as the War was over.

Of course he had indulged in a number of fiery, passionate affairs.

They did not last long, but were the talk of all the gossips while they continued.

When he had met Fleur Munroe he broke all his rules and found a proposal of marriage trembling on his lips within three weeks of their first encounter.

Fleur was older than the usual *débutante*.

She had not appeared in London until she was nineteen, as she was in deep mourning for her Father.

She was lovely.

The fact that she had been left a large fortune was, as far as the Marquis and a number of other men were concerned, immaterial.

He thought, as soon as they met, that there was a rapport between them.

They were drawn to each other like magnets.

Secrecy was, Fleur assured him, absolutely essential.

Nothing must be known by anybody until the last month of her mourning came to an end.

"You know how shocked everybody would be," she said in a low voice, "if I announced my engagement before I have taken off the last of my mourning clothes and started to wear bright colours."

The Marquis had understood.

She had come to London sooner than she should have done only because she was to make her curtsy at the first Drawing-Room of the Season to be held at Buckingham Palace.

It would, he knew, be thought an insult to the Prince Regent to change it.

Fleur had insisted, therefore, that the Marquis behave as casually as possible when they met in public.

But if he crept into the house unseen, then they could be together in private.

The Marquis found it refreshing to find a woman who did not boast about her conquest from the first moment he cast an eye in her direction.

It fact, he rather enjoyed slipping into the garden in Park Street, where Fleur lived.

She would open the long French windows on the Ground Floor to let him in.

Then he would kiss her until they were both breathless.

They would plan their future life together until she sent him away.

"I am fed up with all this secrecy," he had said only two nights earlier. "I love you, my Darling, and I want the whole world to know that you are mine."

"And I love you," Fleur said softly. "You are so handsome, so clever, and so much better at everything than any man I have ever known!"

"In future," the Marquis had said, "you will know as few men as possible. It drives me mad to see you dancing with all those fools when you might be with me."

He paused to kiss her before he continued:

"If I ever thought you were listening to their words of love, I would put a bullet through their heads!"

"Oh, Johnnie, Johnnie! How masterful you are!" Fleur murmured. "But you know, if I am to be your wife, it would be a great mistake to have people saying unkind things about me."

She gave a little sigh.

"I am afraid some people are jealous."

"Of course they are, because you are so beautiful!" the Marquis said, as was expected of him.

But he found it was easier to express himself in kisses than with words.

When he left her because she said she had to dress for a dinner-party, her eyes were shining.

She looked so lovely, it was almost impossible for him to tear himself away.

She let him out of the house by the same window through which he had come.

As she did so, she said in a whisper:

"Be very, very careful! It would be such a mistake if anybody talked about me."

"You can trust me, my Darling."

He had crossed the garden quickly.

He let himself out through the door into the Mews with the key which Fleur had given him.

Only as he was walking back to his own house in Berkeley Square did he realise he had forgotten to ask her to which dinner-party she was going.

If it was before a Ball, he was quite certain he would have been invited to it and he could look in later.

At least he would have a chance of dancing with her.

Then he remembered that if he danced with an unmarried girl, the gossips' tongues would undoubtedly wag.

They never stopped talking about him as it was.

If there was the merest hint of marriage plans in the air, they would be agog.

"I had better go to the Club," he told himself.

He was disregarding at least five invitations his Secretary had left on his dressing-table so that he was compelled to see them.

He had, however, seen Fleur at two Balls the past week.

Now, as he thought of it, he realised she had been dancing with the Earl of Settington, who was heir to the Duke of Dorset.

He was rather a plain young man whom the Marquis had seen at Race-Courses when his father was running a horse.

And he was often unpleasantly drunk at White's.

Neither he nor Charles accepted him as one of their friends.

It had never struck him for one moment that he might be a "runner-up" where Fleur was concerned.

There were a number of other men he knew who were pursuing her.

But they had not his position in life, his wealth, nor his reputation of being a sportsman.

He was quite certain that they were not the least danger.

But now Perceval, of all people, knew about him and Fleur.

What was more, he had dared to assume that Fleur was looking for a bigger title than his own.

It all passed through the Marquis's mind, and he was aware that his friend was looking at him apprehensively.

"Whatever you may feel about this, Johnnie," he said, "you cannot make a scene in here."

"I have no intention of doing so," the Marquis replied, "but I want to know the truth, the whole truth, Charles, even if I have to squeeze it out of you!"

"I knew you would be angry," Lord Charles said unhappily.

"Of course I am angry," the Marquis said, "and I want your reassurance that this is not true."

"I am afraid that is something I cannot give you."

"You mean—it is?"

"I am afraid so."

"How do you know for certain?"

The Marquis felt he was like a man clutching at a straw to save himself from drowning.

He could not believe—it was impossible for her to do so—that Fleur had been deceiving him.

How could she have falsified her protestations of love and the way she had surrendered herself to his kisses.

As if he were reading his thoughts, Lord Charles said:

"From what I hear, Fleur does love you, and she has never cared for anybody else, but she cannot resist the chance of being a Duchess."

"How do you know all this?" the Marquis enquired testily.

Lord Charles hesitated for a moment, then he said:

"As it happened, my Mother's Butler is Uncle to Perceval's Valet."

"Good God!" the Marquis exclaimed. "Not more servants' gossip?"

"You know as well as I do," Lord Charles replied, "that servants belonging to the best families are handed down from generation to generation, and their children, their Cousins, and, I suppose, their grandchildren all find places with the aristocracy. Although you may dislike Perceval, his Family Tree is almost as long as your own!"

"I have always heard that servants were the worst snobs on earth," the Marquis said, "but I never really believed it."

"That is because you do not have to engage them yourself," Lord Charles replied, "but your Secretary

12

will tell you how he scrutinises every reference before any newcomer is privileged to cross your threshold."

Lord Charles could see that the Marquis was listening, and he went on:

"Your staff is mostly supplied from the villagers on your Estate, and they are trained from the age of twelve to look up to you in awe and admiration!"

"Oh, shut up!" the Marquis said.

At the same time, he knew his friend was talking sense.

Now, as he thought about it, he realised that the same families had occupied positions at Eagles, his family seat, for generations.

He remembered when he was a small boy his Father taking him into the different departments to see the Carpenters, the Stonemasons, the Wood-Cutters, and the Painters.

The indoor staff had totalled over fifty then and now.

"We are a State within a State," his father had said, "and you must always remember, Johnnie, that they are your people and you have to look after them, care for them, and prevent them where possible from making mistakes."

It was something, once he inherited, the Marquis had always tried to do.

He had been, as Wellington had said in one of his Despatches, a brilliant Commander.

He looked after his troops and cared for them in the same way as he cared for his Gamekeepers, his gardeners, his grooms, and his jockeys.

Now it struck him that perhaps they were gossiping about him in the same way that Perceval's Valet was doing.

"What makes me furious," he said aloud, "is that I

have always trusted my servants. It never struck me that anything I said at my Dining-Table or to my Valet when I was dressing would be repeated outside."

"I think you are rather naïve," Lord Charles said. "Of course they talk, and they would not think it at all disloyal if they talked to their brothers, their sisters, their Cousins, or any of their relatives, because they were part of the family."

"Well, all I can say is, if this goes on, it is a miracle to me we ever have any National secrets left!"

Lord Charles laughed.

"You must be aware, Johnnie, that Napoleon had spies everywhere, and when he got them into a Nobleman's house, he learnt far more than snooping about round the Ministerial Offices!"

"Is that really true?" the Marquis asked.

"One of the footmen at Carlton House was a spy," Lord Charles said. "It was all hushed up, but not before Napoleon had learnt a great deal from the indiscreet conversation of the Regent's guests before he was discovered and eliminated."

"But that is terrifying!" the Marquis exclaimed.

"I am sure a great many battles are lost and troops killed through careless conversation while the servants are listening!" Lord Charles remarked.

The Marquis did not reply, and after a moment he continued:

"My Father used to say people assumed servants were deaf and dumb, but strangely enough, they are human beings like everybody else!"

"I was just thinking," the Marquis said, "of the conversations that have taken place at Eagles and in Berkeley Square which were certainly not meant for any ears but mine and the few guests who could be trusted!"

"But the Butler and the footmen who waited on you undoubtedly listened at doors, and enjoyed such revelations!" Lord Charles remarked.

"I do not believe you!" the Marquis exclaimed. "You are making it all up!"

"I wish I were," Lord Charles replied, "but the truth is that as far as Perceval's bet is concerned, Fleur will accept your proposal only if the Duke rallies and lives on for a few more years."

The Marquis sat up in his chair.

"I will call, and have the truth out of her!"

"She will deny it—of course she will deny it," Lord Charles said. "But quite frankly, Johnnie, it will not do any good and only upset you more than you are already."

"Upset? Of course I am upset!" the Marquis snapped.

He picked up his glass of champagne, then put it down again.

"Getting drunk is not going to solve anything," he said. "I have to reason this out."

Lord Charles looked at him sympathetically.

He did not, however, say anything until the Marquis, in a different tone of voice, asked:

"What am I to do, Charles? You know that if the Duke rallies and Fleur marries me, I shall never believe in her again. I think actually I would hate her for destroying my ideals."

"I suppose what you are saying," Lord Charles replied, "is that you want to be loved for yourself, and not for your Title or your possessions."

"Of course that is what I want!" the Marquis agreed. "Do you suppose I have not been aware that every ambitious Mother with a marriageable daughter has been stalking me for years?"

He paused before he said:

"When I think of the way they are paraded before me like Yearlings in the Spring Sales, I cannot think how I could have made such a fool of myself!"

"You have every excuse," Lord Charles said sympathetically. "Fleur is very lovely, and also very clever."

"Clever enough to deceive me!" the Marquis said bitterly. "I believed her—really believed her, Charles!"

"You have to face the fact," his friend answered, "that it is very difficult for any woman to see you without the glitter of a coronet and the sun shining on hundreds of windows at Eagles!"

"Are you seriously telling me that no one will ever love me for myself?" the Marquis asked.

"Of course they will love you," Lord Charles answered, "you have had enough proof of that already. But what you are really asking is if they would marry you if you were just an ordinary man with no assets except your face and personality."

The Marquis thought for a moment before he said:

"Yes, that is true, and I suppose it is what every man wants—to be loved as a man and for no other reason."

Lord Charles smiled.

"Why not put it to the test?"

"What do you mean by that?"

"Why not see what the world is like if you were just 'Mister Snooks,' and not the Most Noble Marquis of Mounteagle."

"I refuse to have a name like 'Snooks'! " the Marquis retorted.

"You can call yourself anything you like," Lord Charles replied. "Listen, Johnnie, I will make it a bet!"

He thought before he said slowly:

"I bet my horse *Silver Falcon*, which you admire, against your stallion *Tempest* that you will not be an ordinary man for two weeks without throwing in the towel because you prefer your life as you are living it now."

"Good Lord, Charles, that is not much of a bet! Of course I could be an ordinary man and not miss all the trappings. We put up with enough discomfort, you and I, when we were in the Peninsula."

"You were still a Commander, still giving orders, still admired by your men and, for that matter, by the Generals!"

"All right, how much more uncomfortable do you want me to be?"

Lord Charles thought for a moment before he replied:

"You have just admitted you know nothing about servants. What about being one for the two weeks? Of course it is part of the wager that you must not be sacked for incompetence."

"How dare you suggest that I should be sacked for incompetence!" the Marquis said. "A servant's life is not a difficult one!"

"That is what you think because you have never been one," Lord Charles retorted. "I cannot see you cleaning the silver as well as Mullins!"

Mullins was the Marquis's Butler at Eagles and was well-known to all his friends.

"If I have to be a servant," the Marquis said, "I would rather have something to do with horses. At least nobody could fault me there!"

"That is true," Lord Charles said. "It is giving you an unfair advantage, but I will allow you to be a Coach-man."

"That is something, at any rate," the Marquis said. "I

have always admired *Silver Falcon*, and will certainly enjoy putting him in my stable."

"You are flattering yourself!" Lord Charles said. "And I will ride *Tempest* with the greatest enjoyment."

They both laughed, and the Marquis poured Lord Charles another glass of champagne.

Then, as he put the bottle back into the cooler, he said:

"You are not serious?"

"Why not?" Lord Charles asked. "After all, if you see Fleur, you are bound to let her know what you are feeling, and you have to admit if you have learnt the truth from servants' gossip, it will put you on a par with Perceval."

The Marquis's lips tightened.

"That is the last insult," he said, "and something I have no intention of doing!"

"Very well, accept my bet, and let us put it in the Betting Book."

The Marquis reached out towards the Betting Book which was lying on the chair next to him.

Then he changed his mind.

Instead, he said:

"It will make people curious, and the one thing we have to swear on everything we hold Holy is that nobody else has the slightest idea of this."

He gave a short laugh that had no humour in it.

"Can you imagine how the gossips would enjoy such a tale? We would never be able to live it down!"

"That is true," Lord Charles agreed, "and I promise you, Johnnie, I will not talk."

"Nor shall I," the Marquis said, "and now that you have made my flesh creep, I shall never look at a servant again without thinking he is a spy!"

"It will give you a chance to find out how the other half lives," Lord Charles said.

He was, in fact, although he did not wish Johnnie to know it, very relieved that the Marquis had not taken the truth about Fleur Munroe more violently.

The Marquis had been more in love than he had ever known him to be before.

Therefore, he had been afraid that he would "throw discretion to the wind" and call Perceval "out."

In that way he would precipitate a scandal which would electrify the whole of London.

Because he had been so brave during the War, the Duke of Wellington had praised him on every possible occasion.

The Marquis was therefore admired by a great number of people whose opinions were respected.

He was envied only by those who knew they could never emulate him.

Lord Charles had always suspected that Fleur Munroe was too good to be true.

He was appalled when he learnt that she was meeting the Earl of Settington in exactly the same way as she was meeting the Marquis.

His first impulse had been to inform his friend immediately of her treachery.

He was, in fact, grateful that he had been spared this by Perceval's bet.

However, he knew that the Marquis was deeply hurt.

It would take a little time for him to recover from what he would always think of as a woman's perfidy.

The best thing he could possibly do was to go away.

Then out of the blue had come the idea of him impersonating a servant.

Lord Charles thought it would certainly keep his

mind off the woman who had betrayed him.

Perhaps, at the same time, it would give him a new insight into the lives of those who were not as comfortable as himself.

The Marquis had everything.

It would be difficult, Lord Charles thought, for him to understand that other people suffered in a hundred different ways, ways about which he knew nothing.

He had admired the Marquis ever since they had been at Eton together.

There he had excelled at every sport and, most unfairly, some thought, carried off many of the intellectual prizes as well.

"He was not born with a silver spoon in his mouth," Lord Charles told himself, "but one encrusted with diamonds!"

"Now, let us think this out, Johnnie," he said aloud, "and the first thing, as you well know, will be to find you a situation. For that we shall have to forge you references."

The Marquis, who had been looking somewhat despondent, cheered up.

"We will work the whole thing out exactly as if it were a campaign," he said.

"That is something you always enjoyed doing," Lord Charles reminded him.

"I suppose in a way I shall enjoy this," the Marquis said, "but my disguise must be foolproof."

"Of course!" Lord Charles agreed. "Otherwise you will lose your bet, and *Tempest* will be mine!"

"Damn you!" the Marquis cursed. "You are too cocksure! If I cannot be a very capable and commendable coachman, then I shall be very ashamed of myself!"

He smiled before he added:

"If you remember, Charles, I was a jolly good actor when I was at Eton. You cannot have forgotten those Shakespeare Plays we were made to perform? I was an excellent Shylock!"

"I thought actually you were better as Bottom in *A Midsummer Night's Dream*!"

"Now you are deliberately insulting me," the Marquis objected, "and I have a good mind to make you come with me as my underling!"

"That would be a mistake," Lord Charles said quickly, "because I would try to ensure that you did not succeed in taking *Silver Falcon* from me!"

"The whole idea is mad!" the Marquis said. "Let us have another drink on it!"

Lord Charles raised his glass.

"To the best-looking Coachman who has ever tooled a Four-in-Hand!" he said.

"I prefer to think I am the most efficient with the reins!" the Marquis retorted.

Then, as he drank his champagne, he asked himself how the Devil had he been talked into doing anything so foolish.

chapter two

BACK in his house in Berkeley Square the Marquis sat down to plan out what he should do.

He realised that Charles was right in thinking he should leave London.

It would be a mistake to meet Fleur.

At the same time, although he felt he hated her, some part of him, which he supposed was his heart, still longed for her.

She was so lovely, soft, and amenable.

He could hardly believe that beneath that beautiful facade there was a crafty, scheming, social-climbing woman.

He found it impossible to sit still.

He got up to walk round his Study, which was lined with books.

He was, although most people would have been surprised, an avid reader.

He had a sudden impulse to go abroad and visit the far-off places he had never seen.

Then he told himself he had no intention of letting Charles have *Tempest*.

"I will win *Silver Falcon* first, then, if I find I cannot face Fleur, I will explore parts of the world I have only read about."

He sat down at his desk and rang the bell.

A footman answered immediately.

"I wish to see Walters," the Marquis said.

"Very good, M'Lord."

The footman left him to go, the Marquis knew, through the door at the back of the house which led into the Mews behind it.

Walters was his Coachman in London.

He was a young man compared to the Chief Coachman at Eagles, who had worked in the stables for thirty-two years.

While he was waiting, the Marquis drummed with his fingers on the desk.

But his brain was working as it had been when he was planning a campaign for his troops against superior Napoleonic forces.

He had been so successful in War that he had surprised himself as well as those in command.

At least then, he thought, he had been in charge and knew who his enemy was.

It was certainly not a pretty face with a lying tongue and huge eyes which hid the truth.

It was only a short time before the door was opened, and the footman said:

"Mr. Walters, M'Lord."

The coachman came into the room.

The Marquis looked at him in a different manner from that which he normally used.

Walters was a tall man, almost as tall as himself.

Although his features were somewhat coarse, he was undoubtedly good-looking and had dark hair which was swept back from a square forehead.

He stood respectfully just inside the door until the Marquis said:

"I wanted to see you, Walters."

"Aye, M'Lord?"

"Come nearer, because what I have to say is confidential," the Marquis said.

Walters moved until he stood in front of the desk at which the Marquis was sitting.

"A friend of mine," the Marquis began slowly, "has taken a wager worth a considerable sum, and he needs your help."

Walters looked puzzled, but he did not speak and the Marquis went on:

"He bet another friend that he would drive a Four-in-Hand, at which he is an expert, as an ordinary Coachman for two weeks, without anybody being aware that he is in fact a Nobleman."

Walters was listening, and the Marquis was aware there was a glint of comprehension in his eyes.

"Now, what I want you to do to help my friend," he said, "is to obtain a position for him as a Coachman."

" 'Ow can Oi do that, M'Lord?" Walters enquired.

"It should not be difficult," the Marquis replied, "I suppose you know of a Livery Stable or an Agency where most Society people engage their servants?"

"Oi do, M'Lord. It be Hunt's in Mount Street. Us got a driver there temp'ry when Bill were kicked by one o' t'horses."

"I remember that," the Marquis said, "although I had no idea from where you had obtained the man."

" 'E weren't bad," Walters said, "an' Oi thinks Mr.

Barrett give 'im a good reference when 'e leaves us."

Mr. Barrett was the Marquis's Secretary.

The Marquis had no wish for him to know about the bet.

Barrett was quick-witted and might guess that the Marquis was somehow involved.

"Now, what I am saying to you," the Marquis said, "is entirely confidential. I am trusting you to tell no-one, and by that I mean *no-one*, what I am asking you to do for my friend."

"Oi'll not say anthin', M'Lord," Walters replied, "but Oi don't know wot Yer Lordship be askin' me t'do."

Slowly and painstakingly, so that there would be no mistake, the Marquis spelled it out in words of one syllable.

Walters was to go to the Agency and ask for a job for himself.

"You will explain," he said, "that you are only my second Coachman and the Coachman over you is still young enough to be driving my horses for a long time."

He paused and then continued:

"You therefore want to be a Coachman, a situation to which you feel your experience entitles you."

"Oi understands, M'Lord," Walters said, "but if it gets about Oi be lookin' for another post, people'll think as Yer Lordship's dispensin' with me services."

"They are not going to think that," the Marquis said, "because you will not use your name."

"Not use me own name?" Walters repeated in astonishment.

"No, of course not!" the Marquis replied sharply. "You have never been to an Agency before, because, if I remember rightly, you have been in my employ since you were a stable-lad, then a groom, and finally

26

a second coachman, so they are not likely to recognise you."

"No, 'course not, M'Lord."

Walters looked more cheerful.

Then he asked, as the Marquis expected:

"Wot name should Oi give, M'Lord?"

"I have been thinking of one," the Marquis answered, "and it should be something simple. What about 'John Lyon'?"

"Sounds all right t'me!" Walters grinned.

The Marquis had deliberately used his own Christian name, thinking if he was addressed quickly, he might easily forget to reply.

He also reasoned that he might give his name without attending properly to what he was saying.

By the time he got to his surname, he would remember he was in disguise.

He had tried to think of all the pitfalls into which he might fall.

He had noted that Walters was slow and also thought before he spoke.

"That is what I must do," he told himself.

"You are quite certain, Walters," he said, "that you can do this now—this afternoon—and make sure that nobody else in the house or in the stables has any idea where you have gone."

"Oi sometimes go out for a walk on me own, if Yer Lordship ain't give me no orders," Walters replied.

The Marquis supposed he visited a Public House in Shepherds Mews, or a Tavern in Hertford Street which he knew was patronised by a number of Coachmen.

He said aloud:

"I have no orders until this evening, so go at once and see what you can find out for me."

He suddenly wondered what he would do if there were no vacancies.

He took out a piece of his crested writing paper from the leather holder on his desk and put it down in front of him.

Picking up a freshly sharpened quill pen, he wrote a glowing reference for "John Lyon."

This man, he said, had been in his service for over two years, and he continued:

*"He is an honest, satisfactory, excellent
man whom I do not hesitate to recommend
for a position higher than he occupies at
the moment."*

He signed his name, sanded it, then passed it to Walters.

As he did so, he knew from the way Walters looked at it that he could not read.

He put out his hand and took it back.

"I will read you what I have written, Walters," he said, "and I can only say that if you ever wish to leave my employment, I will write an even better one for you!"

"Oi'll not be a-doin' that, M'Lord!" Walters said as he grinned. "Not 'til Oi be too old t'see the road in front o' me!"

"And by that time I shall be too old to write your reference." The Marquis smiled. "How old are you, by the way?"

"Thirty-five, M'Lord."

As the Marquis was three years younger, he thought he had made a good choice in selecting Walters to represent him.

He sent the man off with instructions for when he returned.

He was to ask to speak to him with the excuse that it concerned one of the horses.

He knew that otherwise, the household would think it strange that he was seeing Walters unless there was a good reason for it.

"Oi'll remember that, M'Lord," Walters said as he left the Study.

He shut the door behind him.

Only then did the Marquis wonder if perhaps the Butler or any of the footmen had been listening at the door.

The idea had never crossed his mind before, and it annoyed him that it should do so now.

"I shall never feel the same about my servants in the future!" he told himself angrily.

He had always been extremely proud of how proficient they were and how smoothly everything ran in all his houses.

He knew that a great deal of it was due to Mr. Barrett.

At the same time, it was also, as Charles had said, because his servants all came from families which succeeded each other from generation to generation.

To be knife-boy at Eagles was a prized position.

Every village lad aspired to it when he reached the age of twelve.

The girls wanted to be Under-Housemaids.

They wept their eyes out when there was no vacancy at the Big House.

Then they had to seek employment elsewhere in the Country or, worse still, in London.

Walters had been gone only a few seconds when the

Marquis opened the door of his Study.

He looked at the footmen who were on duty in the hall.

He thought if he found them whispering together he would know they were discussing what they had just overheard by eavesdropping, in which case his secret was already out.

To his relief they were standing stiffly on either side of the front-door.

They were not speaking to each other, but merely looking bored.

He shut the door again.

At the same time, he was incensed that he should have been suspicious and angry that his peace of mind had been disturbed.

He was sure he would never feel really safe again.

He would be on his guard whether he was making love to a pretty woman or discussing secret information with the politicians he often entertained.

"The whole thing is preposterous!" he told himself.

His logical mind asked him what was the alternative?

To do without servants was unthinkable.

Two hours later he was beginning to think that Walters must have failed.

Then the door of the Study opened, and Hanson, his Butler, said:

"If 'tis convenient, M'Lord, Walters'd like to speak to Your Lordship about *Red Star*."

"*Red Star*?" the Marquis exclaimed with well-acted surprise. "I hope there is nothing wrong with the horse!"

"That might be th' reason, M'Lord."

"Then you had better send him in!" the Marquis ordered.

A minute later Walters came into the Study rather red in the face, but obviously pleased with himself.

Before he could speak, the Marquis put his fingers to his lips.

He walked across the room to stand at the window that was farthest from the door.

Then he beckoned Walters to join him.

When they were standing nearer to each other the Marquis said:

"Keep your voice low. I do not want us to be over-heard."

" 'Course not, M'Lord."

"You have been successful?"

"Aye, M'Lord, an' Oi thinks it's an excellent job fer the gent'man!"

"What is it?" the Marquis asked.

Walters felt in his pockets and rather clumsily brought out a piece of paper on which was written:

> "Lady Horncliffe,
> Islington House,
> Islington Square."

The Marquis scrutinised the name, thinking with satisfaction that he had never heard of Lady Horncliffe.

"You say you got this job?" the Marquis enquired.

"Oi has, M'Lord. They engages Oi right away as 'Er Ladyship's coachman's broken 'is leg."

The Marquis nodded, and Walters went on:

"Th' Sec'tary tells Oi 'Er Ladyship be leavin' for Herefordshire first thing to-morrow mornin' an' Oi'm t'be at t'Mews eight o'clock sharp!"

The Marquis repressed an exclamation of surprise. At

31

the same time, he was delighted.

This was certainly much quicker than he had dared to expect.

It meant he would be gone from London before anyone realised it.

He would leave Charles to find excuses for his absence.

He knew too that it would puzzle Fleur, and he only hoped she would be worried.

Then he forced himself to think of what Walters was saying.

"As it be a long distance, M'Lord, 'Er Ladyship's travelling wi' four 'orses in a closed carriage. Th'luggage be going in a Brake wi' six 'orses an' leaving early."

He paused for breath, then added:

"There be two Out-riders, M'Lord."

"Her Ladyship obviously travels in style!" the Marquis remarked.

He was still racking his brains, thinking he had never heard of a "Lady Horncliffe."

As it happened, he knew no-one in Islington.

It had recently become a fashionable part of London.

"While you were there, Walters," he asked, "did you learn anything about Her Ladyship?"

"On'y that 'er be very rich, M'Lord, but not too easy wi' th' money!"

The Marquis smiled.

It was just the sort of information he would need, and he enquired:

"Anything else?"

"Th' Sec'tary don't say much, M'Lord, but th' grooms say as 'ow they be glad they're not goin' on t'journey, as even a little o' 'Er Ladyship goes a long way!"

The Marquis laughed.

"I am sure my friend will be very grateful to know what you have found out," he said, "and it will make it easier for him to play his part as a Coachman."

"Oi 'ad a good look at t'horses, M'Lord," Walters said. "There be nothin' wrong wi' them!"

The Marquis thought that, at any rate, was a relief, but he did not say so.

"I know what a good judge you are, Walters," he said, "and when it comes to horses, no-one could 'slip a fast one' past you!"

"Oi hopes not, M'Lord, and Oi thinks as 'ow the gent'man who'll be drivin' 'em'll find 'em easy to 'andle, if they moves as good as they looks."

The Marquis made a note of this information, then thanked Walters again for helping him.

"My friend will be very grateful for your assistance," he said, "and he asked me to give you this."

He put three guineas into Walters's hand, and his eyes lit up as he took them.

"That be generous, real generous, M'Lord, an' Oi thanks th' gent'man an' wishes 'im luck!"

"I think he will need it!" the Marquis remarked. "But remember—if you say one word and his disguise is penetrated, he will be disqualified and lose his bet!"

"Oi'll be silent as t'grave!" Walters promised.

The Marquis began to turn away, and Walters said: "Ye'll let me know, M'Lord, if 'e wins?"

"Of course I will," the Marquis answered, "but that will not be for two weeks."

"Oi understands, an' thank ye, M'Lord!"

Walters touched his forehead and left the Study.

The Marquis studied the piece of paper containing Lady Horncliffe's address.

"Eight o'clock to-morrow morning," he told himself, and put it into his pocket.

Then he sent a messenger to Lord Charles's lodgings to say he expected him for dinner.

He had made no plans for the evening because he did not know at what time Walters would return.

If he had failed at the Agency, he would have had to send him to other places in London.

Now he wanted to talk to Charles and not sit alone with his thoughts.

He looked at the clock.

He was already half-an-hour late in visiting Fleur at her house in Park Street.

She would be waiting at the window to see the garden gate open.

She would wonder what had kept him and why he had not let her know he would be late.

When they wished to communicate with each other, he sent her a note addressed to her maid.

Jones was the only person, Fleur had assured him over and over again, who had any idea what they felt for each other.

Now it was infuriating to know that Jones had been relaying everything they did to Perceval's Valet.

"Damn the woman! She is as treacherous as her mistress!" the Marquis said to himself.

Several times during the day he had wondered if the Duke had died.

If he had, would Fleur tell him by letter or by word of mouth that they were no longer engaged?

It hurt him unbearably to think of her surrendering herself to Settington's kisses as she had to his.

Did she tell him in that soft, sweet, innocent little voice that she loved him?

Would Settington evoke the same little tremors in her body that he had been able to do?

"Curse her! She will haunt me for ever!" the Marquis said savagely. "And I will never, never be able to trust any woman again!"

He would have been a fool if he had not been aware of the social consequence to him.

He knew what it would mean to any woman to be the Marchioness of Mounteagle and wear the superb family tiara at the Opening of Parliament.

He had always thought that when he had a wife, she would grace his table as his Mother had done.

He could remember as a small boy peeping at her from the Minstrels' Gallery.

When there was a big party at Eagles she looked like the Fairy Queen.

She had been very beautiful with diamonds glittering on her head and round her neck.

He had gazed at her in rapture, which was what he also did when she came to his bed-room to kiss him good-night.

"Is it a very, very big party to-night, Mama?" he remembered asking on one occasion.

"Very big, Darling," his Mother had said, "and Papa's guests include a King and Queen from overseas, and the Prime Minister of England."

"I would like to have dinner with you," the Marquis had said.

His Mother hugged him. Then she said:

"One day, darling boy, you will sit in Papa's place and I hope you will have a wife, who is very beautiful and who loves you very much, sitting in my chair."

"She could never be as beautiful as you, Mama!" the Marquis had said loyally.

His Mother laughed.

"I hope she will be more beautiful and love you as much as I do!"

She had kissed him good-night and he had lain awake for a long time.

Now, he told himself, his Mother's wishes would never come true.

Women would want to marry him because he was sitting in his Father's place.

She would sit in his Mother's chair with her tiara on her scheming little head.

"I will never marry!" he vowed.

He spoke the words aloud, and thought as he did so that he challenged not only Fleur but all women.

Then he knew despairingly that sooner or later he would have to take a wife.

He must have an heir who would become the next Marquis and carry on the family tradition.

He would accept the traditional practices of those who had a title.

When the present Lord Lieutenant of Oxford retired, he would succeed.

He was already Gentleman-in-Waiting and Honorary *Aide-de-Camp* to the Prince Regent.

Every Marchioness of Mounteagle became a Lady-of-the-Bedchamber.

There were a dozen other posts to be filled automatically simply because he had stepped into his Father's shoes.

Of course he wanted to have a son who would step into his shoes when the time came.

But for the moment he shrank from the whole idea of marriage.

It was just as he shrank from women because even to

look at one would remind him of how Fleur was trying to trick him!

And how she had lied and lied and lied.

He was still walking up and down his Study when the footman returned with a note from Lord Charles.

It said he would be with him just before eight o'clock.

The Marquis went upstairs to change his clothes.

His Valet was waiting for him.

He was again a family servant who had started life at Eagles and had begun to Valet him as soon as he left Eton.

He would have liked to have his Batman, who had been with him in Portugal and France, as his Valet.

But he had known it would cause a deep feeling of resentment.

How could a stranger be appointed to what was considered one of the most important posts in the household?

The Marquis had therefore had to say good-bye to Hawkins and had rewarded him with a pension for life.

He also found him employment with one of his friends who was not encumbered by such a large number of family servants.

His present man, Storton, was excellent at his job and, the Marquis had always thought, extremely loyal to him.

Now he asked himself if Storton was to be trusted.

If he was walking out with the lady's-maid of some Society Beauty, everything he overheard would be repeated.

Because the mere thought of it made him angry, the Marquis undressed and had his bath in a stony silence.

It made Storton look at him apprehensively.

He did not understand what was worrying his master.

It suddenly struck the Marquis that it was likely Storton knew about Fleur!

Therefore, if he appeared depressed or incensed, it might seem suspicious.

"Oh, my God!" he said to himself. "Where does this tangle end, and will it be possible for me ever to be natural again?"

He remembered that Storton had no idea he was running away.

With what was a tremendous effort, he said casually as he stepped from his bath:

"Oh, I forgot to tell you, Storton! I am going off to the country for a day or two with Lord Charles. He wants me to see some horses which he thinks are an excellent buy, but it would be a mistake for the owner to know who we are."

Storton looked at him in surprise.

"How's Your Lordship going to prevent 'im from doin' that?" he enquired.

"He is apparently quite a simple man of little importance, but sharp when it comes to the price for what he has to sell."

Storton grinned.

"All o' them be like that, M'Lord!"

"I know," the Marquis agreed, "pack me just a few things that I shall require, but nothing oversmart, do you understand?"

"Yes, o' course, M'Lord. And when'll Your Lordship be leavin'?"

"At about seven o'clock to-morrow morning," the Marquis replied, "so call me an hour earlier. Lord

Charles is picking me up, and, of course, you will not be coming with me."

"Sorry 'bout that, M'Lord."

"I expect you will find something to do in my absence," the Marquis remarked.

He thought as he spoke that Storton smirked and was quite certain there was a woman he was seeing.

He longed to ask if she was a lady's-maid, and who was her mistress.

Then he knew it would be a mistake to ask leading questions which might be remembered afterwards.

"Pack everything to-night," he said as he finished dressing, "and, of course, I will not take my leather dressing-case or anything with my crest on it."

"I'll be careful o' that, M'Lord. But you'll of course want your ridin' things?"

"Yes, of course," the Marquis agreed, "and in case we have to be out in all weathers, I had better take my tiered driving-cape."

"As Oi've already told Your Lordship, it's gettin' shabby!" Storton said.

"All the better on this journey," the Marquis said, "but remind me to order a new cape when I get back."

"I'll do that, M'Lord."

The Marquis walked downstairs.

Charles would be waiting for him, but he had already decided that if they were going to talk, it would be a mistake to do so in the house.

The servants might listen at the door after they had withdrawn into the Study.

'I feel as if I am living in a foreign land,' he thought. 'Never before in my whole life have I suspected anyone around me, mistrusted every woman, or felt a man with a higher title than my own is undoubtedly my enemy.'

As he entered the Study, Charles was waiting for him.

He thought, as the Marquis came into the room, that it was the first time he had ever seen a cynical twist to his lips.

*   *   *

The Marquis arrived at the Mews of Horncliffe House at seven o'clock the next morning.

Charles had arranged, as they had agreed, to convey him there in a Hackney Carriage.

It seemed abysmally slow after his own spirited horses.

"Is there any news?" the Marquis asked when his friend picked him up in Berkeley Square.

Lord Charles did not pretend that he did not know about whom he was speaking.

"Settington came into the Club when you left," he replied, "and I heard somebody ask him how his Father was."

"What did he reply?" the Marquis enquired.

" 'Not any better,' Settington said, 'but we have not given up hope.' "

The Marquis thought spitefully that that would keep Fleur guessing.

She would undoubtedly try to get in touch with him.

She would want to find out why he had not kept his appointment with her as he had promised.

"What are you going to say when Fleur, and, of course, a number of our other acquaintances, ask where I am?" he asked Lord Charles.

"I have not really decided," Lord Charles replied.

"Perhaps that you have gone to the country—not to Eagles but to one of your other houses because you have been informed there has been a burglary there."

"What are they supposed to have taken?" the Marquis asked.

"That is immaterial," Lord Charles replied. "Everybody is afraid of being burgled, and before I can talk about your troubles they will be speaking of theirs and telling me of their safety precautions."

The Marquis laughed, but it was not a particularly spontaneous sound.

"In other words, you do not think anybody is going to worry about my absence?"

"Only Fleur, and if the Duke does recover, she will be frantic to get hold of you!"

"Then keep her at bay until I return."

"And what are you going to do then?" Lord Charles enquired.

"I have not yet decided," the Marquis answered, "but I might go abroad."

"Do you want me to come with you?"

"Of course! And I thought we might explore parts of the world we have never seen."

"I must say, it is something I have always wanted to do," Lord Charles replied, "but I have never been able to drag you away from your beloved Eagles, and the horses, which I often think mean far more to you than any woman."

"That is what I thought until I met Fleur," the Marquis replied.

"You have to forget her," Lord Charles said quietly, "and having been through the same misery myself, I can only say that time heals."

"I suppose you are right," the Marquis agreed, "but

41

it is damned painful until it does."

"I know," Lord Charles said, "but think how much more painful it would have been if you had found all this out after you had married her!"

The Marquis knew that what he was really implying was that Fleur would be unfaithful, and that unless he wanted a scandal, there would be nothing he could do about it.

"You are right," he said after a pause, "and I am well aware, Charles, why you are sending me off on this 'wild-goose chase'!"

He paused and then continued:

"But, if you ask me, my body is going to feel the discomfort of it while my mind will be still suffering from shock."

"Cheer up, old boy!" Lord Charles replied. "You may find it quite an adventure, and I have never known you not to take your fences in style, or funk one!"

The Marquis laughed.

"All right, Charles, you win! I know you are trying to dig me out of my slough of despond, but to tell the truth, I feel the whole thing is dirty and unpleasant."

"Of course it is!" Charles agreed. "But actually, I am thanking God that I was able to save you."

"You are a good friend," the Marquis said, "and perhaps one day I will be grateful for this mad, and, I cannot help thinking, extremely foolish escapade!"

The Hackney Carriage drew up at the top of the Mews.

Lord Charles bent forward and opened the door.

"Good luck, and take care of yourself! If it is too unpleasant, you can always 'throw in the sponge'!"

"What? And let you have *Tempest*? I will be damned if I do!" the Marquis responded.

Lord Charles laughed.

The sound followed the Marquis as, carrying his luggage, he walked down the Mews.

He was wearing his driving-clothes and over them his many-tiered driving-coat.

Storton might think it looked shabby, but it had been cut by a Master Tailor.

In fact, the Marquis looked very smart with the tall hat he wore a little on the side of his head, and his polished boots.

It was very much the same as those worn by his coachmen, and which had just come into fashion.

The servants of the Dowagers and more elderly of the aristocrats were still wearing the boat-shaped hat.

It was the same as the hat that was drawn on Napoleon Bonaparte's head in every caricature.

The Marquis had all those that belonged to his livery destroyed as soon as he returned from the War.

The only difference between his hat and that of this coachmen was that Walters wore a cockade in the front of his.

A cockade was permissible only when the owner of his servants' livery was entitled to a crest.

As the Marquis had no idea whether or not Lady Horncliffe had one, he could not therefore be expected to arrive with a cockade already on his hat.

In fact, before he left his employer, who was supposedly the Marquis of Mounteagle, he would have been obliged to surrender it in the same way the footmen would surrender their striped waist-coats and their jackets with the silver buttons bearing the Marquis's crest.

Walters had told the Marquis that Lady Horncliffe's stable was half-way down the Mews.

" 'Tis painted a deep green, M'Lord, an' there be

stalls wi' at least a dozen 'orses."

The Marquis had no difficulty in finding the place.

He pushed open a door and saw four grooms staring at him with enquiring eyes.

" 'Marnin'!" he said, trying to speak with a slight accent. "I be John Lyon, an' I thinks you're 'spectin' me."

"Glad to see yer!" the oldest groom exclaimed, holding out his hand. "Ye've come at t'right moment, 'Er Ladyship's wantin' t'leave early, an' us were 'alf-afraid t'horses would 'ave to drive orf withou' ye!"

He laughed at his own joke, and the Marquis managed to laugh too.

" 'Ow long 'ave I got?" he asked.

"Aw, it'll be orlright," the other man exclaimed. "It's allus t'same wi' 'er. Gives orders at night an' cancels 'em th' next day, 'til ye begin t'wonder if ye're on yer 'ead or yer 'eels! As ye'll soon find oot!"

"Sounds difficult," the Marquis replied, "but I suppose it's always the same with elderly women!"

The groom stared at him. Then one of the others said:

"Wot makes yer think 'Er Ladyship be elderly?"

"I thought she must be," the Marquis replied, "after what you said."

The grooms all laughed.

"Well, ain't ye in fer a surprise!" the oldest groom remarked. " 'Er be no more'n twenny-five if 'er be a day! An' pretty as a picture in a frame o' gold! Wot more can ye ask?"

The Marquis smiled.

"You've certainly surprised me!" he said.

chapter three

THE Marquis drove the carriage, which he could see was new, expensive, and well-sprung, round to the front-door.

From the moment he picked up the reins he was aware that the horses were exceptionally good and that he would enjoy driving them.

At the front-door there was a red carpet, four foot-men in gold and crimson livery, and a general atmosphere of tension.

The Marquis realised the cause of this when he heard a shrill, hard voice talking inside the house.

Somebody was being given orders and at the same time told off for some wrong-doing.

He guessed the voice was that of his employer.

He was wise enough not to turn his head but to look straight ahead.

He lowered his chin to make sure the high collar of his cape partially obscured his face.

Then he realised that a man was speaking to him from below.

One quick glance told him this was the Secretary who had interviewed Walters.

"Here are your instructions, Lyon," he was saying, "I suppose you can read?"

"Aye, Sir."

The Marquis mumbled the words, hoping they sounded like Walters's rather thick articulation.

"Her Ladyship requires you to drive quickly but safely. Take no risks."

"I'll not do that, Sir."

He took the sheets of paper that were handed to him and glanced at them.

He realised that, as he had expected, he would be taking the road out of London which eventually would lead them to Oxford.

As he had been a student there for three years before he joined his Regiment, he knew the road well.

He thought that as the weather was fine, it would be in fairly good condition.

The footman who would sit beside him on the box was standing at the horses' heads, a precaution against them trying to move off before Lady Horncliffe was properly settled inside the carriage.

Without appearing to do so, the Marquis moved his head slightly.

He was able to see Lady Horncliffe as she emerged from the entrance hall.

The grooms were right—she was pretty, but in a flamboyant manner.

Her golden hair had touches of red in it, she had two large blue eyes in an oval face.

Her lips owed their colour to a crimson salve.

She was dressed to attract attention with a high-peaked bonnet festooned with small ostrich feathers.

The sunshine glinted on the jewels in her ears and at her neck.

The Marquis quickly looked away.

He was smiling, however.

He thought that Charles would doubtless be amused when he learnt what his employer looked like.

Lady Horncliffe stepped into the carriage giving a series of orders to the Secretary in her sharp voice.

She was followed by another woman.

Once they were seated and the rugs were arranged over their knees, a footman shut the door.

It was a signal for the man holding the horses to clamber up onto the box beside the Marquis as quickly as he could.

Then, as the Secretary, the Butler, and the footmen all bowed, they drove off.

The Marquis had not driven far before the footman beside him, whose name he remembered was Jack, said:

"Oi 'opes ye knows th' way. 'Er gets reet furious if us goes wrong."

"I knows the way," the Marquis replied.

He glanced at his instructions again before he put them back into his pocket.

He saw there was a stop for luncheon at what he guessed would be a Posting Inn.

It was about fifteen miles away.

As they had left punctually, he reckoned he could cover the distance easily.

He would not therefore be in trouble for being late.

The sun was shining, and there was a crispness in the air which he appreciated.

He therefore settled himself down to drive the horses and enjoy himself.

He was glad that he had not to be shut up inside a carriage, which he always disliked.

At least he had chosen a job that enabled him to be in the fresh air.

Once out of London and in the countryside, because he was curious, he said to Jack:

"Have you been with Her Ladyship a long time?"

"Two year, 'though it seems longer 'cause 'er be a real devil when roused!"

The Marquis was amused.

"What's happened to her husband?"

" 'E be dead. That's why 'er comes t'London."

"I imagine he were older than she is," the Marquis remarked after a moment's pause.

" 'Ow d'yer guess that?"

"And I suppose he were rich."

"Nay, t' was 'er as 'ad th' money."

The Marquis found this surprising.

But as the horses were gathering speed, he had to concentrate on them.

He thought he would learn more later on.

The Out-riders had kept behind the carriage as they drove through Islington Square.

Now, as there was no traffic, they rode on the fields on either side of the road.

Both, the Marquis noted, were young men.

The horses they were riding were as well-bred as those he was driving.

"She certainly has good taste in horses!"

He was speaking his thoughts aloud rather than directing them at the man beside him, but Jack replied:

"They ain't be of 'er choosin'. T'were th' Master as knew a good 'orse when 'e sees one. 'E 'ad 'is own

48

'ounds when 'e were young."

The Marquis thought he was gradually piecing together a puzzle.

It would eventually complete the picture that was forming in his mind.

They reached the Posting Inn just beyond Uxbridge.

He drove the horses with a flourish into a large yard, and brought the carriage to a standstill.

Jack jumped down to open the door.

The Marquis wondered whether his employer would comment to him on his driving or tell him of anything he had done wrong.

But Her Ladyship swept into the Inn, where a bowing Landlord awaited her.

She was followed by her companion, who, the Marquis noted, had a young and slender figure.

He, however, had seen only her back view, and not her face.

He glanced again at his instructions.

They were to change horses—which had obviously been sent ahead—to-night at a Posting Inn called The Dragon. It was, if he remembered rightly, near High Wycombe.

All he had to see to at the moment was that the horses were watered and out of the sun.

"Are you feeling hungry?" he asked Jack. "Is there something for us to eat?"

"There'll be summat," Jack replied, "but not much. 'Er don't pay 'nough."

The Marquis raised his eyebrows.

It was usual for an employer on a long journey to provide the Coachman and Out-riders not only with good food, but with ale both at luncheon and supper.

He, however, made no comment but told the ostler from the Inn to keep an eye on the horses.

He then followed the other three men, who had already gone inside.

He found them in a small, dingy room which was kept for visiting drivers.

The Marquis knew from his own experience that Lady Horncliffe would be given a Private Parlour.

Other travellers would eat in the Dining-Room.

The three men were sitting at an old table.

On it the Marquis saw a hunk of cheese, a loaf of bread, and a pat of rather dubious butter.

"Is that all we get?" he enquired as he sat down.

"That be all 'er pays fer!" Jack replied.

One of the Out-riders, whose name the Marquis learnt was Ben, cut himself a hunk of cheese.

"Oi be that 'ungry!" he said plaintively.

"Now I think of it, so am I!" the Marquis replied. "And I will see what I can do about it."

He went from the room and found the Landlord just coming from the Private Parlour.

As he met him, a mob-capped maid passed, carrying a large tray on which there was a whole salmon and stuffed goose.

Another maid followed her with two roasted chickens and a boar's head.

The Inn-keeper, seeing him eyeing the food, said sharply:

"Oi puts on yer table what be ordered!"

"I know that," the Marquis replied, "but we have come some distance, and have another fifteen miles to go. You will appreciate we are all comparatively young men, and we are hungry!"

The Inn-keeper shrugged his shoulders.

"Oi've had me orders!"

"Bring me a ham, a tongue, and the boar's head if Her Ladyship doesn't want it. I'll pay the difference," the Marquis said.

The Inn-keeper looked at him in surprise.

"So yer're free with yer money!" he remarked. "Ah, well, t'be none o' my business!"

"None," the Marquis agreed, "except I want the best meat and not what's been refused by your other customers!"

The Inn-keeper gave him a sharp look as if he intended to say something rude.

Then he obviously thought better of it.

Despite himself he was impressed by the Marquis's appearance.

"Ye get what ye pays for!" he said in a somewhat surly manner.

He walked off towards the kitchen.

A maid carried in a ham from which very little had been cut, and a cold turkey.

Later, after it had come from the Parlour, the boar's head appeared, which delighted the Out-riders and Jack.

"That be real kind o' ye," Ben said. "Oi feels a new man!"

He certainly looked better, the Marquis thought.

He was less "pinched" looking about the face, which he was sure was due to the boy being under-fed.

It made the Marquis angry that anybody should be so mean.

He was insistent that anyone in his employment should have good food and enough of it.

He paid for what they had consumed and also for the jugs of ale he ordered for all of them.

He had made friends, and their attitude towards him changed.

He was aware when they had first seen him that they were slightly hostile.

Because his appearance was so different from theirs, they had thought, as Charles would have said, that he was "up to something."

Now he had shown himself to be one of them.

They talked to him freely.

They appreciated his cleverness when he told them that he had money because he had backed a horse that had won at Epsom earlier in the Week.

"If Oi puts so much as a penny on a 'orse," Jack said, " 'e falls at the first fence!"

"The next time I get a good tip," the Marquis replied, "I'll tell you about it, but betting's usually an easy way of losing!"

"So's makin' love!" Ben quipped. "But who's agoin' to say no!"

They all laughed at this.

Then Jack looked at the Marquis and said:

"Time be gettin' on."

The Marquis realised that because he was the Coachman it was up to him to get them all ready before Lady Horncliffe appeared.

He was sitting on the box and the Out-riders were mounted when she stepped through the door.

The Marquis expected her to get straight into the carriage as she had before.

To his surprise, however, she came to the front and, looking up at him, said:

"I am in a hurry to reach my destination which is on your list of instructions. Therefore, do not dawdle on the way!"

The Marquis touched his cap with a finger but did not speak.

After a moment she said even more sharply:

"You understand what I am saying? If you were a more skilful driver, we would have got here a quarter-of-an-hour earlier!"

Again the Marquis touched his hat but did not reply.

With a flounce of her skirts and a toss of her head, Lady Horncliffe got into the carriage.

As the door shut, Jack climbed up beside the Marquis and they were off.

The Marquis realised she had found fault for the sake of doing so.

He therefore drove the horses not only faster than he had done during the morning, but also fast enough to swing the carriage.

It was something he personally most disliked.

They reached the village of High Wycombe, where they were to stay the night, in record time.

The Posting Inn was quite impressive, but not as large as the one at which they had stopped for luncheon.

As the Marquis drew the horses to a standstill in the yard, the Inn-keeper appeared at the door.

Jack scrambled down.

As Lady Horncliffe stepped out of the carriage, she came to the front to say:

"Too fast and too dangerous! If you drive like that, you will soon be looking for other employment!"

She did not wait for the Marquis to speak or even to touch his cap.

She walked into the Inn.

An ostler showed them the stables at the side of the yard.

The Marquis saw the stalls were comparatively clean and the straw fresh.

The Out-riders stabled their horses, then came to help with those which had drawn the carriage.

The Marquis had always looked after his own Charger during the War.

He did not trust the troopers, who often were very ignorant where horse-flesh was concerned.

He therefore helped remove the harness of the horses he had driven and rubbed them down.

He made sure the fodder they had brought with them filled their mangers.

Then he checked that the water in their pails had been newly filled from the pump and had not been left standing.

As Ben came up to him in a friendly fashion, he remarked:

"I suppose you are hungry again!"

"Oi be ready t'eat an ox!" Ben replied.

The Marquis laughed.

"Then let us go and see if we can find one!"

They went into the Inn.

They found they were to be accommodated, as they had been at luncheon, in a room especially provided for servants.

There were two other coachmen there, but they left soon after the Marquis arrived.

"Oi wonder wot we're gonna 'ave," Ben remarked hopefully.

He was soon to be enlightened.

An elderly maid who looked rather harassed slapped a tray down on the table.

It contained a small amount of boiled mutton and a dish filled with badly peeled potatoes.

"Be that all?" Ben asked.

There was a loaf of bread that was stale, but nothing else.

Ben and the others looked disappointed, so the Marquis said:

"I will see what I can do."

When he provided a hare soup which was surprisingly edible and a large portion of pork, he thought that he had never known his guests to be so grateful.

'Charles would certainly laugh at what is happening!' he mused.

He finished before the others and rose to his feet, saying:

"I think I will take a stroll and look at the horses before I go to bed."

"Bed!" one of the Out-riders exclaimed. "Ye'll not find one o' them in th' loft!"

The Marquis stood still.

"The loft?" he questioned.

"That be where us sleeps," the other Out-rider explained. "An' Oi only 'opes there be plenty of 'ay. Th' last time I travels wi' 'Er Ladyship, there weren't enough t'cover em ankles!"

The Marquis did not say anything, and walked out of the room.

He went to the stables and saw that the horses were perfectly all right.

Then he walked round the garden of the Inn.

Charles or no Charles, he was not going to sleep in the loft.

Anyway, it was something he never asked his own servants to do.

When he got back to the Inn, there was no sign of Ben or the others.

He took the Inn-keeper to one side.

"I am not feeling very well," he said, "I think I have a cold coming, so I would like to have a bed-room to myself, which, of course, I will pay for."

The Inn-keeper was about to tell him he should sleep in the loft with the other servants.

Then, as he looked into the Marquis's eyes, he thought better of it.

"T'll cost ye half-a-guinea, if ye've got it!" he said.

The Marquis drew the coin from his pocket and put it down on the table.

"I want a comfortable bed," he said. "I can see you are not full."

Again the man hesitated.

Then he told one of the maids to show the Marquis the way upstairs.

He brought his leather case which had been put under his seat on the carriage.

They climbed, not to the top floor as he had expected, but to the first and walked along a corridor to the end.

The maid, who was a middle-aged woman, opened the door and said:

"Ye'll be comfortable enough 'ere, but I be surprised at th' Master a-letting ye 'ave it!"

"I am a privileged person!" the Marquis replied.

"I 'spect that's what a lot of women tell ye!" she answered with a flash of humour he had not expected.

He saw that the room was clean and tidy.

The bed looked comfortable.

"Thank you," he said.

He wondered if he should tip her, but thought that would seem strange on the part of a servant.

Instead, he smiled at her again.

There was an undoubted look of admiration in her eyes before she shut the door.

She had carried a candle to guide them upstairs and left it on the dressing-table.

Now the Marquis lit another from it.

He wondered if Charles would think he was breaking the rules by not joining the others in the loft.

"I cannot think why I agreed to this ridiculous bet!" he told himself.

The answer made him think of Fleur.

He went to the window and pulled back the chintz curtains.

Outside, dusk had fallen and the stars were already coming out in the sky.

It made him remember how he had kissed Fleur only two nights earlier in the garden behind her house.

She had come with him as far as the door which led out of the garden into the Mews.

They had spent nearly two hours together in the Sitting-Room.

He had felt then that no-one could be more soft, sweet, or adorable.

He had kissed her until the blood was throbbing in his temples, and his body burnt with the fire of desire.

Then, when they had reached the door leading out of the garden, he had once again pulled her close against him.

"How can we go on like this?" he asked fiercely. "Let us get married immediately—to-morrow—and I will teach you, my darling, about love!"

"That is what ... I want," she had whispered, "but we have ... to wait ... we have ... to!"

It was an argument they had had over and over again.

Because he knew words were useless, he had kissed her passionately and demandingly.

Finally she had drawn away from him and almost pushed him through the door into the Mews.

He had gone away, his head in the clouds.

He wanted her, he thought, as no woman had ever been wanted before.

Now he knew she had just been waiting to see whether the Duke lived or died.

"Damn her!" he swore beneath his breath. "Damn her! Damn her!"

Suddenly there was the explosive sound of a door being slammed.

He was aware that somebody had come into the room next to his.

The Inn was old and he could hear quite clearly somebody running across the room.

Then he heard the person, whoever it was, fling themself down on the bed, which creaked.

The Marquis turned from the window.

He suspected it must be a man who had drunk too much and was therefore incapable of undressing.

He hoped that his neighbour, drunk or sober, would not be noisy.

He was just about to take off his coat when he heard a sound that surprised him.

Yet it was unmistakable.

He listened.

The newcomer was crying.

It was not anything soft and gentle, but something tempestuous, despairing.

The Marquis listened again and knew he was not mistaken.

Only a woman who was stricken in some way would

cry so unrestrainedly and so pathetically.

There was nothing hysterical about it; it was the sobbing of utter misery.

On an impulse he opened his door.

He took a few steps down the passage and knocked on the one next to it.

It was a very soft knock, as if he did not want to be overheard.

The sobbing did not cease and he turned the handle of the door.

It opened and he saw the room was almost a replica of his own.

Lying on the bed, crying convulsively, was the figure of a young woman.

There was one candle burning on the dressing-table by which he could see the back of her head.

Her whole body shook as she cried.

He stood looking down at her, aware that she had not heard him.

Then, leaving the door ajar, he walked a little nearer to the bed.

"Can I help you?" he asked.

As he spoke, he was aware that the woman stiffened, and she stopped crying.

"What can have upset you?" the Marquis asked quietly.

She raised herself to look at him with what he knew was sheer astonishment.

Her eye-lashes were wet and tears were swimming in her eyes which seemed to fill her small face.

The hair which framed it was so fair as to be almost as silver as the starlight.

She raised herself on one arm and now she stared at him as if it were hard to focus her eyes.

Then, as her vision cleared, she was astonished by his appearance.

"Who . . . who are . . . you?" she asked through lips that trembled.

"I am in the next room to yours," the Marquis explained, "and I felt I had to ask why you were so unhappy, and if perhaps I could help in some way."

"No . . . no-one can . . . h-help me," she answered in a voice that was almost incoherent, "b-but . . . I am s-sorry if I . . . woke you."

"You did not wake me." The Marquis smiled. "I have not yet gone to bed."

He thought as he looked at her that he had never seen a woman who could look so lovely when she was crying.

Her tears seemed to enhance her beauty rather than detract from it.

She put up her left hand to wipe her eyes as a child might have done.

The Marquis took a fine linen handkerchief from his pocket and held it out to her.

She sat up straight before she took it from him.

Then, as she wiped her eyes, she said in a trembling voice:

"I . . . I am . . . s-sorry."

"There is nothing for you to be sorry about," the Marquis said. "Tell me what is troubling you."

"I . . . I do not . . . know what . . . to do," she said. "What can I do?"

She was speaking, he realised, as if to herself, and she went on:

"I . . . I was so . . . certain . . . she would . . . understand . . . and I could . . . keep . . . Peter with me . . . but now . . ."

The tears ran down her cheeks again.

Holding the handkerchief with both hands, she put it over her eyes.

The Marquis realised there was a chair near the bed, and he sat down on it.

"Now, stop crying," he said, "and tell me what all this is about. It is always upsetting to see a pretty woman crying."

The girl, because she was nothing more, took the handkerchief from her eyes and stared at him.

Then she said:

"I . . . I know who you are . . . you are the new . . . coachman! But . . . why are you . . . here?"

It was then the Marquis was aware who she was.

He had seen only her back when she walked into the Posting Inn behind Lady Horncliffe.

"I am here," he answered, "because I did not feel well enough to sleep in the loft as my companions are about to do, and I therefore took a room which I am paying for myself. I can only beg you will not give me away, as it might cause trouble."

"Of course . . . I will not . . . say anything," the girl agreed, "and . . . Papa would never have . . . approved of the Coachmen or the Out-riders . . . not being . . . properly looked after."

"I agree with your Father," the Marquis said, "and I am sure he would not wish you to be as upset as you are now."

The girl shut her eyes.

"Papa is . . . dead," she said, "but he would understand . . . why I . . . am so . . . unhappy."

"As your Father is not here to advise you," the Marquis suggested, "why not tell me what is wrong? Perhaps I can find the answer."

The girl made a helpless little gesture.

Then she said:

"N-no-one can . . . h-help me . . . except . . . Lady Horncliffe . . . and she has . . . refused!"

"Refused—to do what?" the Marquis enquired.

"Refused to let . . . Peter . . . stay with me."

The words seemed to burst from between the girl's lips.

Then she said in an agitated, frightened voice:

"How . . . can I let him be . . . sent away to an . . . Orphanage because . . . there is . . . nothing else . . . and I promised Mama I . . . would look . . . after him . . . but I have no . . . money and she will not pay me for . . . what I do."

It all sounded very incoherent, and the Marquis said gently:

"Suppose you start from the beginning and, first of all, tell me what is your name, what you are doing here, and why Lady Horncliffe will not let you have Peter with you?"

With what he knew was a commendable effort at self-control, the girl wiped her eyes.

Then she looked at him and said:

"Perhaps I . . . ought not to be . . . talking to you . . . like this."

The Marquis smiled in a manner which most women found very beguiling.

"Who is to know," he added, "except perhaps the stars and the mice in the wainscotting?"

"You . . . will not . . . understand," the girl said, "but as you say . . . no-one . . . will know."

"What is your name?" the Marquis asked.

"It is . . . Laela Horn."

He raised his eye-brows.

"You are a relative of Lady Horncliffe, for whom I am working?"

"Papa was a . . . distant Cousin of her . . . husband's."

"And you say your Father is dead?"

"Papa . . . died of his . . . wounds nearly . . . two years ago."

"His wounds?" the Marquis questioned.

"Papa was a sailor. He served under Lord Nelson, and eventually was Captain of his own ship."

There was a note of pride in Laela's voice which the Marquis did not miss.

"And he was wounded."

"He engaged two French ships and defeated them both," Laela replied, "but a cannon-ball shattered one of his . . . legs and he very . . . nearly . . . died."

She gave a little sob before she said:

"Mama and . . . I nursed him . . . and he lived . . . for nearly two years."

"And where did you live?" the Marquis asked.

"We went to many places," Laela answered. "Mama fell in love with Papa when his ship was patrolling the coast of Scotland."

There was silence, as if she were looking back at what had happened, until the Marquis said:

"So they were married."

"Yes . . . but only . . . after Mama's Father had . . . forbidden her to marry . . . a Sassenach and said he would . . . never speak to her again if . . . she did so."

"But she defied him," the Marquis said, feeling he must have heard this story somewhere before.

Laela nodded.

"They were married, and Mama followed Papa to whichever Port his ship went. I remember a little house we had at Portsmouth and another at Plymouth. But of course he was away at sea for months and months, and Mama was always . . . afraid he would be . . . killed by . . . the French."

"What happened after he was wounded?" the Marquis asked.

"He was invalided out of the Navy and, when he came back to England, Mama had no idea where they would live. So she wrote to Sir Laurence Horn, who was a distant Cousin."

The Marquis was listening interestedly as she went on:

"He lived in a dear little village in Kent, and because he felt sorry for Papa, he gave us a small house on his Estate, where we were very, very happy."

"Then what happened?"

Laela looked away from him and said in a different tone:

"Sir Laurence . . . was . . . married!"

The Marquis waited, already guessing the answer.

"He had never been married . . . before," Laela went on, "because he had served in India and other parts of the world, and had never found time to . . . settle down."

She gave the Marquis a wistful little smile as she added:

"But he . . . longed to . . . have a . . . son."

"So he married the Lady you are with now," the Marquis suggested.

Laela nodded.

"She was so . . . pretty besides being very . . . very . . . rich."

"But, surely, much younger than him?"

"Yes, of course, but her father, Mr. Cliffe, had made a huge fortune in shipping."

The way she spoke, and also his intuition, told the Marquis how the fortune had been made.

It was in the same way as a number of other Liverpool magnates—by shipping the slaves from Africa to America.

It was something he had always abhorred.

He knew that the Ship-owners obtained large fortunes by kidnapping the wretched black men, women, and children who lived near the coast.

They carried them in stinking holds to the New World across the ocean.

America needed them to work in the cotton fields.

"So Mr. Cliffe wanted his pretty, rich daughter to become 'respectable,' " the Marquis said.

"H-how did you . . . guess that?" Laela questioned.

"It is something that has happened before," the Marquis replied, "and I suppose he insisted that his own name was added to 'Horn.' "

"Mama told me that he was very insistent about that, although I know Papa was . . . rather shocked."

"And did Lady Horncliffe produce the much-wanted son?" the Marquis enquired.

Laela shook her head.

"No . . . there was . . . no son and I think that is . . . perhaps why she . . . will not . . . let me have . . . Peter with . . . me."

"Peter is your brother?" the Marquis asked.

"Yes . . . he is only . . . eight and such . . . a dear little boy. Everybody . . . loves him, and he is no . . . trouble to . . . anyone."

"What has happened to the rest of your family?" the Marquis enquired. "Your Mother, for instance?"

"Mama . . . died three . . . months ago . . . soon after . . . Cousin Averil . . . decided she would . . . no longer . . . wear mourning because she . . . wanted to go . . . to London."

Now Laela's voice changed and she said:

"It was all . . . terrible! I can not believe how it . . . could have . . . happened so . . . quickly! Just after Mama's Funeral . . . Cousin Averil told me she . . . was selling the house and the Estate and . . . with it our . . . house, which I thought . . . belonged to . . . me."

"So you had nowhere to go," the Marquis said.

"She said because I could sew so well I could live with her as a kind of companion-seamstress."

Laela gave a little sob before she said:

"She told me she was . . . going to London at once . . . and I was to . . . go with her. I thought it was for only a short time . . . so I left Peter with a retired Governess who had been teaching him."

She looked at the Marquis to see if he was interested and said:

"Cousin Averil said she was buying a new house in the Country which would be much, much bigger. That is why we are going to Hereford—to look at one. I thought Peter and I would have a . . . cottage together there . . . but now she has changed . . . her mind."

Laela thought for a moment before she added:

"She never actually said we could . . . be together . . . but I never . . . imagined for . . . a moment she would . . . separate us."

"And that is what you learned to-night!" the Marquis said.

"She was talking about the house we are going to see, and without thinking I remarked:

" 'It will be lovely for Peter, as I am sure there will be horses to ride and lots of things to . . . do in the . . . Country.'"

Laela stopped speaking because her voice was choked with tears.

"And what did your Cousin say?" the Marquis asked.

"She said: 'Peter? What do you mean—Peter? I shall have no room for a boy who should be elsewhere learning how to earn his living!' "

Laela's voice died away, and she put her hands up to her eyes again.

After a moment she said:

"H-how could I . . . lose Peter . . . how can he . . . go into an . . . Orphanage . . . where there would be . . . nobody to . . . love him as Papa, Mama, and I have always done?"

Her voice became smothered by her tears.

Now she was speaking as despairingly as she had cried when the Marquis first heard her.

He thought no-one could sound more pathetic or more unhappy.

After a moment he said:

"I realise this is very upsetting for you, but suppose we try to think it out sensibly and find a solution?"

"There is . . . no solution," Laela whispered. "I . . . I have no . . . money and . . . nowhere to go."

"Surely you must have some relatives?" the Marquis asked.

"Papa always said that his relatives were either sailing the 'High Seas,' or else . . . fighting in some . . . distant land."

"What about your Mother's?"

"As I told you . . . they never spoke to Mama after she married Papa. Her Father, who was a clan Chieftain, was very, very angry that she . . . wanted to leave . . . Scotland."

There was silence, then Laela raised her head to say:

"Thank . . . you for . . . listening to me . . . but you do see . . . there is . . . nothing I can do."

She sounded so pathetic.

At the same time, the Marquis was thinking that Averil Horncliffe was as treacherous and self-seeking as Fleur.

All she wanted was a respectable name by marrying a decent man.

Yet she was not prepared to support his relatives even though she was rich enough to do so.

For a moment his lips were set in a hard line.

There was a cynicism in his eyes which Lord Charles would have recognised.

"Now, listen," he said.

As if it were a command, Laela raised her head to look at him.

Once again he thought it was impossible for anyone to cry so piteously and so violently, and yet still look lovely.

In a way it was as if she were not a human being.

She was made like the Statues of the Saints he had seen in the French Churches after they had captured a village.

The Nuns had tended the English wounded as well as those of their own country.

"I am sure that, if you think this over," he said, "you will find there is something you can do which will enable you to earn enough money to keep yourself and Peter."

Laela made a little murmur, but did not interrupt.

"Until you find out what it is," he continued, "I have an empty cottage to which you can take Peter if your Cousin continues to refuse to let you have him with you."

Laela stared at him as if she could not believe what she had heard.

Then she said:

"Do you . . . mean what you are saying? Is it really . . . true that you . . . have a cottage and it . . . is empty?"

The Marquis was sure there were several on his Estate, and he replied:

"I am quite sure, and to go there at least will give you breathing space."

"And Peter will . . . not have to go . . . into an Orphanage!" Laela said beneath her breath.

Then she clasped her hands together and said:

"How can you be . . . so kind . . . so wonderful? Are you . . . quite . . . quite sure you . . . can afford . . . it?"

"I am quite sure," the Marquis said, "and anyway, the rent for a small cottage is not very large."

"I promise you . . . I will try to make enough . . . money to pay you . . . what I owe," Laela said. "I can really sew quite well, and I am sure there will be people who will buy things from me, if I can have time to find them."

"The cottage is yours when you want it," the Marquis said. "Now go to sleep, and do not worry any more."

"I cannot believe what you are . . . saying is . . . true!" Laela cried. "When I left Cousin Averil I was so . . . upset that I just . . . ran from the room . . . feeling that everybody, including Papa and Mama, had . . . forsaken me."

"I am sure wherever they are they would never do that," the Marquis said. "Now, stop being unhappy and just remember that at the end of this journey there will be a place for you and Peter to be together."

"I . . . I do not believe you are . . . real," Laela said. "I think you are . . . an Archangel sent . . . down from . . . Heaven especially to . . . help me!"

"Shall we say it is a very good thing I was next door?" the Marquis replied. "And remember, that is a secret between us."

"Yes, of course. Would I do . . . anything so . . . wicked and . . . wrong as to . . . betray you when . . . you have been . . . so kind?"

"No, I am sure you would not," the Marquis said.

He rose to his feet and, pushing back the chair, said:

"Go to bed and remember, the sun will be shining to-morrow, and Peter will be waiting for you to collect him."

"Promise you will not . . . disappear and will be . . . here . . . to-morrow to tell me . . . where your . . . cottage is?" Laela begged.

The Marquis laughed.

"I will not disappear, and we will talk again when the opportunity arises. But you do realise that nobody must know you have been talking to a mere Coachman?"

"The kindest and most understanding Coachman in the whole world!" Laela replied.

The Marquis smiled at her and walked across the room.

As he reached the door, Laela said:

"Thank you . . . thank you . . . again and again!"

The Marquis let himself out and automatically looked to see that no-one was in the corridor to notice him.

There was nobody about, and he went quickly into the room next door.

He thought as he undressed that this strange encounter was something which would intrigue Charles when he heard about it.

'This is certainly something I never expected on my first night as a servant!' he thought before he went to sleep.

chapter four

THE luggage was brought out to be put at the back of the carriage.

The Marquis had learnt from Jack that this was the last night they would stay at a Posting Inn.

"The Brake be gone on to t'Big House where we be stayin'," he said, "an', thank th' Lord, we'll not be sleepin' in th' loft!"

"Was it uncomfortable?" the Marquis asked sympathetically.

"There weren't much hay, an' wot there were was full o' insects!" Jack said disgustedly.

As the Marquis was about to climb up onto the box, Laela came through the door.

She was looking, he thought, even lovelier in the daytime than she had at night.

She looked at him shyly but with an expression of gratitude in her eyes that was unmistakable.

He deliberately did not smile at her, and she put some things she held in her arms into the carriage.

Then she stood waiting for Lady Horncliffe to appear.

When she did she looked, as usual, spectacular.

The Marquis realised that despite the small amount of luggage they carried she had a different bonnet from the one she had worn yesterday.

The Landlord, bowing and scraping, was exclaiming what an honour it was for him to have Her Ladyship at his Inn.

Lady Horncliffe made no reply.

She got into the carriage, the door closed, and the Marquis drove off.

He had looked at his directions after what Jack had said.

He felt much relief that this was indeed the last night of the whole journey they would spend at a Posting Inn.

The following day they would be at Crowstock Towers.

He realised that to reach it they would go north of Oxford.

This meant it was not so far across Country from Eagles.

There was a danger that somebody he knew would recognise him.

It did not say in his directions to whom the house belonged.

He racked his brains to recall if he knew anybody by the name of Crowstock.

After they had gone some distance, he asked the question of Jack.

"The gen'man's name be Crow," Jack replied, "an' as 'e's a friend of 'Er Ladyship, ye can bet 'e'll be rich!"

The Marquis now had the answer to his problem.

Sir Percy Crow was a man he had heard of before because he was so enormously rich.

He was self-made and, having received a title for his very generous contributions to Party Funds, had been awarded a Knighthood.

A great number of people had thought this was a disgrace, and had not hesitated to say so.

Percy Crow had tried to become a member of White's Club and failed.

Then he had put forward his name for Boodle's, and was immediately "blackballed."

Disappointed that he could not be accepted by the *Beau Ton* of London, he had then moved to the Country.

He bought a large Estate.

It had belonged to a Nobleman who had become impoverished during the War, and whose son had been killed fighting the French.

Sir Percy had promptly changed the name of the house.

He proceeded to try to become a "Country Gentleman."

The Marquis could remember hearing how he had tried to buy himself the position of M.F.H.—Master of the Fox-Hounds.

He had also contributed over-generously to every possible Charity.

A few of the younger people in the County had more or less accepted him.

The older generation had shaken their heads and refused every invitation he sent them.

'Well, one thing is for certain,' the Marquis thought as he drove on, 'none of my friends will be at Crowstock Towers!'

They paused for luncheon and, as usual, the Marquis provided extra food to the delight of Ben and the others.

They reached the outskirts of Oxford at five o'clock.

The Marquis drew up his horses at a black-and-white Posting Inn which he remembered.

It was called the Three Bells.

He found, after he had entered the court-yard, that the stables were nearly full.

This was not only with the horses of other travellers, but with the four which belonged to Lady Horncliffe.

These had gone ahead two days earlier.

The Marquis had thought it was high time that he changed horses.

The ones he had driven yesterday were tired after what had been a gruelling day.

The four grooms who were waiting with the new team looked at the Marquis in surprise.

"I hope the horses you have here are as good as these!" he remarked.

The man to whom he was speaking grinned.

"If anythin', they be better," he answered. "Oi picks the best, an' I enjoyed the ride."

"Well, take this lot back slowly," the Marquis replied, "they deserve a rest."

"Oi'll see t'that," the man he was speaking to replied. "Oi enjoys Oxford—Oi've bin 'ere before."

The Marquis could say the same but thought it would be a mistake.

He had decided that he would not join the grooms at supper but eat somewhere on his own.

He remembered there was a rather nice Tavern a little way down the road which he had patronised when he was an undergraduate.

He was careful, however, first to ensure that the horses were properly looked after.

Then he went into the Inn to ask for a bed-room.

The Landlord, impressed by his appearance, explained apologetically that almost every room was full.

However, he found one eventually that was smaller and not so well furnished as the one the Marquis had occupied the night before.

Nevertheless, it was better than sleeping in the loft which he was quite certain would be over-crowded to-night.

He sent a chambermaid for some hot water, washed himself thoroughly, and put on a clean shirt.

Then he walked out of the Inn and found the Tavern he remembered.

It was small, but he was not disappointed with the food with which he was provided.

The bottle of claret that was produced after some discussion was at least drinkable.

He wished he had time to go into Oxford and visit his old College which was Christchurch.

He had enjoyed rowing and the other sports, and also the education he had received.

He had got his Degree and remembered how pleased his Father had been when he had done so.

It was getting late when he walked back to the Three Bells.

He was just about to climb the stairs when the Proprietor came hurrying towards him.

"Ye're wanted in t'Parlour," he said, jerking his thumb towards the corridor that ran past the Dining-Room.

The Marquis thought Lady Horncliffe would have gone to bed by this time.

He somewhat reluctantly turned and went towards the Parlour door.

It was a bore, he thought, to have to listen to her sharp voice when he wanted to go to sleep.

He opened the door of the Parlour.

To his surprise, it was Laela who was waiting there.

She was seated in a chair at the fireside, and when she saw him she jumped up and crossed the room, saying:

"When I heard you were . . . not in the Inn I was . . . terribly afraid that you had . . . gone away!"

"No, I am still here," the Marquis said as he smiled, "but perhaps it is a mistake for you to tell me to meet you here."

He thought as he spoke that perhaps the other servants might somehow become aware of it and thus inevitably talk.

"It was not . . . I who . . . sent . . . for you," Laela said quickly. "I would . . . not have . . . dared to do . . . that."

The Marquis raised his eye-brows, and she went on:

"It is Cousin Averil. She wishes to see you, and when I told her you were out, she said you were to go up to her room as soon as you came in."

"What have I done now?" the Marquis asked in an amused voice.

"I . . . do not . . . know," Laela replied, "but she did not . . . seem angry."

"That is a relief, at any rate!" the Marquis said.

He walked across to the fireplace as he spoke and sat down in an arm-chair.

"Tell me about yourself," he said, "are you feeling happier?"

She had followed him, but, instead of sitting on a chair, she sat down on the hearth-rug at his feet.

"Much . . . much happier," she replied, "only I . . .

still cannot ... believe that ... anyone could be so ... kind."

"Your Cousin may change her mind, then Peter can stay with her."

There was a little pause while Laela looked at the fire before she said:

"You may ... think I am being ... foolish, but if your ... cottage is ... available ... I know that Peter and I would be ... much happier ... there than with ... Cousin Averil."

The Marquis considered this in silence for a moment. Then he said:

"Perhaps it is not just a question of happiness, but of what we might call facilities. Surely, if Lady Horncliffe buys her big house, there will, as you hope, be horses for Peter to ride, and, of course, lots of good food for him to eat."

Laela did not answer, and after a moment he said:

"You do not agree with me?"

"It is ... not that," Laela replied, "but, Cousin Averil is ... very funny about ... small things."

The Marquis waited, and after a moment she explained:

"The old servants who had been with Cousin Laurence for years complained after he married that they did not have the best butter, or fresh milk. It all came from the Home Farm and they thought they were entitled to those sort of things."

"Are you telling me she is penny-pinching?" the Marquis enquired.

Laela looked away from him.

"Perhaps I ... should not ... speak like this to you ... but she ... resents me taking a ... large helping of ... any dish, or eating ... the cakes at ... tea. I do not mind ... but it would be ... difficult to ...

explain to . . . Peter why . . . if they are . . . there, he . . . may not . . . eat them."

"I have heard that rich people often have strange 'kinks,' " the Marquis said, "and I have met a few Misers in my time, but they have all been men!"

Laela sighed.

"She is so . . . rich that it seems . . . strange that such little things . . . should matter."

"Well, the cottage is waiting for you and Peter," the Marquis said.

"That is what I hoped . . . you would . . . say," Laela said with a little sigh of relief. "I have already begun to embroider a piece of muslin which will make a very pretty handkerchief . . . but I do not . . . have very . . . much time to . . . work on it."

"I imagine you are acting as lady's-maid besides being a companion and a seamstress."

Laela gave a little laugh.

"That is true, but Cousin Averil's real lady's-maid is waiting for us at Crowstock Towers."

As she had been talking, the flames of the fire had been glinting on her hair.

The Marquis saw that it was in fact so fair that there was a silvery tinge to it.

It was a colour he had never before seen on a woman, and he thought it very beautiful.

It curled round Laela's oval forehead and against her cheeks which had a translucent quality about them.

She had a little straight nose, perfect features, and huge eyes.

They were the pale green of a mountain stream with a touch of gold in them.

She was, he thought, unique.

He was quite certain that if she were fashionably

gowned and appeared in London, she would be a sensation.

He could only imagine that Lady Horncliffe was so obsessed with her wealth, she was unaware that by comparison she looked tawdry and rather common.

The thought that his employer was waiting for him made him rise to his feet.

"I suppose I had better go upstairs," he said, "and you can show me the way to Lady Horncliffe's room. But I would rather stay here talking to you."

"It has been . . . very wonderful to speak to you . . . even for a . . . few minutes."

Her voice vibrated with sincerity.

The Marquis walked towards the door.

Then, as he reached it, he said:

"I think, in case there is anybody lurking about, it would be a mistake for us to be seen together. Stay here until I have gone upstairs, then slip up to your own room."

"Yes . . . of course," she said. "It was . . . foolish of me not to . . . think of . . . that."

"Just tell me where Her Ladyship's room is," the Marquis asked.

Laela explained that it was on the First Floor, and six doors away from the top of the stairs.

The Marquis left the Parlour, shutting the door behind him.

He climbed up the oak staircase which creaked beneath his feet.

He counted the doors carefully and knocked on the sixth.

He heard Lady Horncliffe's voice reply:

"Come in!"

He opened the door.

To his surprise, she was sitting at the dressing-table wearing an elaborate but somewhat revealing negligée.

It fell open at the front to show a lace-trimmed night-gown.

She turned her head as he came in.

Two candelabra which each held three candles stood on either side of the dressing-table.

The light from them picked out the fiery red of Lady Horncliffe's hair, giving the impression of small flames.

"Shut the door, Lyon!" she said.

He obeyed her, then stood just inside it.

He was aware as he did so that she was appraising him.

It was the same way as a man might appraise a horse in a Sale-Room.

Then she said in a comparatively soft voice:

"I wanted to tell you how well you drove to-day, and to say that I am very pleased that you have entered my service."

It was such a change from the way she had spoken to him before that the Marquis could only look at her in surprise.

After a pause he said:

"That is very generous of Your Ladyship."

She turned round a little on the stool.

"You are a fine-looking young man, Lyon! Can you not find something better to do than to drive horses?"

"It is what I enjoy, M'Lady," the Marquis replied, "and at least I am in the open air."

"I understand you have been out," Lady Horncliffe remarked. "Where have you been? And was she very attractive?"

The Marquis laughed.

"It was nothing like that, M'Lady. I merely visited a

local Tavern to have something to eat, and to drink a glass of claret. I think it might upset you to know that those you employ are badly fed, and not provided, as is usual, with a glass of ale."

"I will remember that is what you like," Lady Horncliffe answered in a low voice.

Then, as she looked at him, the Marquis realised what she intended.

Even as he was aware of it, she made a little movement.

Her red hair which was pinned on top of her head fell over her shoulders almost to her waist.

It was done so skilfully that it seemed as if it had happened by mistake.

Yet the Marquis knew it was deliberately premeditated.

He remembered it happening when he was alone with Fleur.

She had given a little cry of dismay and he had honestly believed at that moment that it was accidental.

Now he knew it was just another of the many ruses a woman employs to attract a man.

Fleur had intended to seduce him, just as Lady Horncliffe was doing at this moment.

For a second everything went red before his eyes.

It was yet another female trick, he thought furiously, to enslave a man.

It was craftily calculated as were a dozen others women used to their advantage.

When Fleur's hair fell from the top of her head, he spread it over her face and kissed her passionately through it.

Because she protested shyly at him doing so, it excited him even more than he was already.

He had really believed she had been embarrassed by the way her hair had slipped out of control.

Once again he felt the anger rising in him—against Fleur and against the woman now looking at him invitingly.

He opened his lips as if to tell her what he thought of her.

Then he remembered that if he did so she would undoubtedly dismiss him and he would lose his bet.

With the quickness of a man who had very often been in danger, he thought of a way of escape.

It came into his mind like a flash of lightning.

Lady Horncliffe rose to walk towards him, her open negligée revealing the diaphanous transparency of her nightgown beneath it.

As she did so, he gave an exclamation.

"A rat, M'Lady!" he exclaimed. "A rat has just run under your bed!"

He moved towards it as he spoke.

Lady Horncliffe screamed.

"A rat! Oh, my God! Kill it! I loathe rats!"

She screamed again and climbed up onto the chair on which she had been sitting.

Holding her negligée tightly round her, she watched him with terror-struck eyes.

The Marquis knelt on the floor and put his hand under the bed.

He felt the softness of a velvet slipper and seized it.

He put it under his coat, making it appear to wriggle as he did so.

Then, holding his coat tightly against him with his other hand, he rose to his feet.

As Lady Horncliffe saw the convulsions taking place against his chest, she screamed:

"Kill it! Kill it!"

The Marquis turned towards the door.

With what was apparent difficulty, he managed to get it open while still holding the wriggling "rat" imprisoned against him.

Then he was outside in the passage and he closed the door behind him.

There was nobody about and, pulling his coat back into place, he walked to the stairs.

He was holding the pink velvet bed-room slipper in one hand wondering whether he should throw it away.

Then it occurred to him that if it was missing in the morning, Laela might get into trouble.

She would be expected to have packed it with Her Ladyship's clothing.

He therefore went down into the hall and, finding the Night-Porter, said to him:

"Will you take this to the bed-room of Miss Horn, the companion to Lady Horncliffe? Tell her it was left by mistake in the carriage and I thought she might need it."

The Night-Porter was an obliging man and promised to take it to Laela at once.

The Marquis then went up to his own room.

He was smiling as he did so.

He had been saved by many different things in his life, but never before by a pink velvet bed-room slipper.

*   *   *

The Marquis slept surprisingly well.

However, he felt a little guilty the next morning when

he saw that Her Ladyship's other employees looked heavy-eyed.

They were also more in need of grooming than the horses.

Because it was not so very long a distance to Crowstock Towers, they did not leave until after half-past-ten.

They proceeded to cross the boundary from Oxfordshire into Buckinghamshire.

They were now in hunting country, and the Marquis knew it well.

But the roads were narrow and twisting.

Even with the fresh horses they could not make the same speed as they had done the previous day.

With what was actually very skilful driving, they arrived at Crowstock Towers just before five o'clock.

Sir Percy's house was very large but of not any particular architectural design.

It had been added to over the centuries.

The Marquis thought it was exactly the type of building that would appeal to a "social climber."

It would certainly impress everybody with his wealth.

There was no doubt that Lady Horncliffe was a very welcome guest.

Sir Percy himself came running down the steps when she arrived.

He embraced her warmly and told her in a loud and somewhat common voice how pleased he was to see her.

He also patted Laela on the shoulder and informed her he had a large number of *Beaux* eagerly awaiting her arrival.

There would, he said, be dancing to-night until she

wore out the soles of her slippers.

The Marquis could not hear what Laela replied to this.

Lady Horncliffe was exclaiming plaintively what a terribly tiring journey it had been.

She was, she told Sir Percy, looking forward to the comfort she knew she would find at Crowstock Towers.

"I have a number of friends who are only too willing to console you," Sir Percy replied.

The Marquis was relaxing as he drove away to the stables.

He was sure she would not worry about him if there were other men to prevent her from feeling lonely at night.

Jack was right, they were to be accommodated within the house.

There was no question, therefore, of anybody having to sleep in the loft.

He was allocated a room in one of the wings where the male servants slept.

It was as far away as possible from the women's quarters, which were on the top floor.

The Marquis was gratified that, because of his position, his room was one of the best and he had it to himself.

He noted, however, that while Sir Percy did not spare the expense, his taste was definitely deplorable.

He had been wise enough to employ the Butler who had been with the previous owners.

They quite obviously considered his present employer an upstart.

The Marquis obtained from him a list of the guests.

He knew the names of one or two of them, but there

87

was no-one amongst them who would be an accepted member of White's.

Nor was he likely to have met them at any of the houses of the exclusive hostesses whose invitations he accepted.

The Marquis found he was expected to eat in the Housekeeper's room.

From a servant's standpoint, it was very luxurious.

Because it was a large house-party with a number of the other guests coming in after dinner, most of the staff were busy.

The supper for the upper-servants was served exactly an hour after the guests had eaten in the Dining-Room.

The Marquis had learnt long ago from his Mother exactly how the staff at Eagles behaved.

In the Housekeeper's room, the Butler sat at one end of the table, the Housekeeper at the other.

The visiting ladies'-maids and Valets took their positions from their employers, the lady's-maid of a Duchess, Marchioness, or Countess sitting on the right of the Butler.

The Valet of the most senior Nobleman was on the Housekeeper's right, and his Coachman was on her left.

The rest of the table was allotted entirely according to the importance of their employers.

The Marquis, therefore, found himself on the Housekeeper's left.

He was not surprised to find the food was as good, if slightly more filling, than what was being served in the Dining-Room.

There were five courses and they were waited on by the under-servants.

There were also wines to drink, and he was quite certain they were Sir Percy's best.

He was not surprised, and it was what he expected, when the conversation comprised the same gossip that was circulating in London.

Instead of coming from above stairs, however, it came from below.

They talked about the King's infatuation with the Countess of Hertford.

Then the Valet regaled them with a story about a Nobleman who the Marquis knew well.

He had been seen climbing down a drain-pipe in Mayfair.

The "Fair Enchantress's" husband had returned home unexpectedly and there was no other way of escape.

There was a great deal of laughter at this.

Then Lady Horncliffe's lady's-maid, whom the Marquis had met only a few minutes before supper was served, said:

"I don't mind tellin' you that My Lady has caused a sensation since she's been in London and the 'Beauties' we hears so much about 'ave 'ad their noses put out of joint!' "

"I think she is very pretty!" the Housekeeper said somewhat primly. "At the same, there's two Beauties I've always wanted to see."

"And who are they?" the Valet asked.

"One be Lady Blessington," the Housekeeper replied, "and the other that Miss . . . er . . . Mun-Munroe—that's it—Fleur Munroe! I hear she be real lovely!"

The Marquis stiffened involuntarily as he heard Fleur's name.

Then another lady's-maid remarked:

"You're right there, Mrs. Field, she's beautiful! An' I can tell you, as we've just come from London, there'll be strawberry leaves in her hair afore the end o' the summer!"

There was a little exclamation round the table, and somebody asked:

"You mean she's goin' t'marry that Viscount Settington?"

" 'Course she is," the lady's-maid replied, "an' a very lovely Duchess she'll make! But he'll have his hands full, as would any man she married."

"Why d'you say that?" Mrs. Field asked. "After all, she's only a young girl."

"Young in years, but old when it come to knowin' what's what!" the lady's-maid replied.

"What d'you mean by that?" someone asked.

"That's tellin'!" the lady's-maid said coyly. "But actually, I lived near her Father an' Mother, an' by the time she was seventeen there was some real 'goin's-on' up at the Manor where they lived."

"Oh, come on, tell us what she did!" another woman said coaxingly.

"Well, 'e were a handsome chap, I can tell you that, an' looked his best astride a 'orse. But 'er Mother would have had somethin' to say if she'd known what was goin' on in the woods!"

The Marquis felt he could bear no more.

He rose to his feet, saying to the Housekeeper as he did so:

"I hope you will excuse me, but I have a headache, and must lie down."

"Oh, I'm sorry, Mr. Lyon!" the Housekeeper said sympathetically. "You go to bed. I 'spect you'll find you'll feel better in the mornin'."

"I am sure I shall," the Marquis replied, "and thank you very much."

He walked to the door and the Butler gave him a friendly wave.

As he walked out of the door he heard one of the women say:

"Now there's a good-lookin' man, if ever there was one!"

He hurried away, finding the nearest door that would take him outside.

It was true his head did ache, but he had a suspicion that it was also his heart.

Everything that had been said about Fleur seemed to ring in his ears.

How could he have been such a fool?

How could his perception and his belief that no-one could deceive him have been proved wrong?

How could he have been taken in by her girlish innocence?

And by her beauty which had seemed so pure and undefiled?

Once again he was hating women almost fanatically, simply because he had been deceived.

As if only by exercising his will-power could he relieve his feelings, he walked into the wood beyond the garden.

The moon was rising high and stars filled the sky—somehow it made him feel better, and his anger gradually left him.

Charles had said, "Time is a great healer."

Time was passing, and he would forget Fleur.

He told himself that never again would he trust a woman.

Never again would he be taken in by an aura of

innocence which, when the truth was known, was dirty and shop-soiled.

The night, the stars, and the trees themselves gradually brought him some semblance of peace.

He turned to walk back, choosing a different way from which he had come.

He found after he passed through the trees there was a shrubbery and he had reached the garden.

As with everything else, a great amount of money had been spent on it.

There was an artificial cascade falling from granite rocks into a stream.

It meandered among exotic plants and through blossoming shrubs, to join a flower-bordered lake.

By now he could hear music coming from the lighted windows.

He hoped Laela was enjoying herself.

If she was going to live in a cottage in a small village, it was unlikely she would attend many Balls.

Nor would she have the money to afford a pretty gown.

'It would be better for her if she could make Averil Horncliffe see sense,' he thought.

He walked on, keeping in the shadows of the large rhododendron bushes which bordered a lawn.

Then he was aware there was a fountain.

In the rays of the moonlight which turned the rising and falling water into rainbows, it was a magical sight.

He was standing in the shadows, looking at it, when he heard a woman's voice saying:

"No! Please . . . no!"

"Now, do not be silly," a man replied. "You know you little girls like it, and I want to kiss you."

"No . . . of course not . . . please . . . I must go . . . back to the house!"

"Not until I have kissed you!"

The Marquis looked through the bushes and knew he was not mistaken.

It was Laela who was protesting while a middle-aged man of somewhat stout build was holding on to her wrist.

His other arm was round her shoulders and he was drawing her towards him.

"Oh . . . please . . . please," Laela buzzed, "I . . . I do not . . . want you to . . . kiss me!"

"I will teach you how to enjoy it," the man answered.

He spoke in rather a thick voice, as if he had been imbibing too freely.

Laela gave a little cry, but it was obvious that her pursuer was strong.

Her efforts to free herself were completely ineffective.

"Now, come along, my pretty one," the man said impatiently, "I am not going to take 'No' for an answer!"

He pulled her roughly against him.

She gave a shrill scream and turned her head from side to side to avoid his lips.

It was then the Marquis acted.

He moved forward and grabbed the man by the back of the collar and the seat of his trousers.

With the strength of a trained athlete he lifted him off the ground and flung him into the fountain.

Laela stared at him, her eyes filling her white face.

"Run!" he ordered.

He had a quick glimpse of a smile before she turned and obeyed him.

Then, as her persecutor, cursing and swearing, pulled himself out of the water, the Marquis disappeared.

He slipped back into the shadows of the bushes from which he had come.

As he walked away, he thought this was another story to tell Charles.

His friend had been right. This journey was full of adventures he had not expected.

He went in through the kitchen quarters.

As he did so, he told himself that when he got the chance, he must talk to Laela.

He must tell her that she must never—unless she wanted this sort of thing to happen again—go into the garden alone with a strange man.

Then the memory of what had been said about Fleur came back into his mind.

He wondered if once again he had been deceived.

Perhaps Laela was not as innocent as she appeared to be.

Then he knew there had been no pretence about the way she had fought against the elderly Romeo.

There had certainly been no pretence in the expression in her eyes when she realised who had come to her rescue.

" 'An Archangel from Heaven!' " the Marquis quoted to himself as he went up the stairs.

He was quite sure, at the moment, that was what Laela believed him to be.

chapter five

THE next day the Marquis learnt there was a local Point-to-Point a few miles away.

He knew at once that this would be dangerous because undoubtedly, some of his friends would attend it.

There would be huntsmen, gamekeepers, and grooms who would recognise him.

Fortunately, when he was worrying about it, he learnt that everybody was going in Sir Percy's own carriages and coaches.

They were to be driven by his grooms.

With a sigh of relief the Marquis waited until they had left, then went to the stables.

He had already made friends with Sir Percy's Chief Groom, who was actually more of a Manager.

With the shrewdness of a businessman who knew how to obtain the best, Sir Percy had engaged a first-class man to buy his horses and to supervise them.

Wainwright was a man he would like to have

employed, the Marquis thought, although in fact he himself knew so much about horses that he did not need anybody else's advice.

He hoped that Wainwright would not go to the Races.

When he entered the stables he found his hopes had not been in vain.

Wainwright was sitting in the Harness-Room, reading the advertisements in one of the Sporting Papers.

He looked up when the Marquis entered and smiled.

"I see the Earl of Maresbrook is selling some of his hunters," he said. "Do you think they're worth inspecting?"

The Marquis remembered that the Earl of Maresbrook was an old man, and his son lived in a different part of the Country.

"I should certainly think it is worth your going to the sale," he replied. "Maresbrook, when he was young, had a reputation for being a hard rider to hounds."

Wainwright smiled.

"I'll take your advice," he said, "and if you're still here, we might go together."

The Marquis thought that was unlikely, but he replied:

"As you may have guessed, I have a favour to ask of you."

Wainwright laughed.

"The choice is somewhat limited, but I'm sure we can find a horse on which you can exercise yourself."

"That is what I want," the Marquis said. "I enjoy driving, but it is not the same as having a spirited animal between one's knees."

"That's what I feel myself," Wainwright said. "Let's go and look in the stables."

They walked down the rows of stalls.

The Marquis said nothing until he came to the horse he wanted.

He was called *Victory* and was an exceedingly fine stallion.

He was higher than average and, from what the Marquis had seen, very spirited and hard to ride.

He looked at Wainwright and said:

"I think you knew all along this is the one I would want!"

"Cost th' Master a pretty penny," Wainwright replied, "and I can only ask you not to damage him or he'll have my head!"

"I will not do that," the Marquis assured him.

"Very well," Wainwright said, "I believe you, Lyon, 'though thousands wouldn't!"

The Marquis laughed a little wryly.

He had a reputation as a horseman and had never thought to have it questioned.

However, as he had the horse he wanted to ride, he was not prepared to quarrel about it.

The grooms saddled *Victory* and the Marquis mounted him.

With Wainwright watching him go, he rode off.

It was a joy beyond words to be free, alone, and riding a magnificent horse.

Victory was trying with every trick he knew to unseat him.

It was exactly what the Marquis wanted at the moment.

He enjoyed the eternal battle between man and animal until *Victory* conceded that his rider was victorious.

He then settled down to gallop as fast as the Marquis could have wished.

He rode out into the countryside, being careful to avoid any villages or places where he might be known.

Finally, and it was long after midday, he went into a small wayside Inn to have something to eat.

He put *Victory* into a ramshackle stable, then sat in a small garden at the back of the Inn.

The Landlord, impressed by his appearance, brought him an excellent meal of cold meats, pickles, Stilton cheese, and some home-brewed cider.

Then he rode on again, turning reluctantly back towards Crowstock Towers.

The afternoon was drawing on.

Even *Victory* was tired by now, and the Marquis took him slowly.

When he was not far from the huge, ugly, over-impressive house, he turned into the woods.

The trees had swept away his anger of the previous evening.

He found now that the sunshine coming through the branches, the moss-covered paths, and the song of the birds raised his heart.

The Marquis was thinking not of Fleur but of the amusing anecdotes he would relate to Charles.

'Perhaps one day I will write a book about it,' he thought.

No-one would believe it had all really happened.

But he imagined that his adventures would at least make those who read them laugh.

He was drawing nearer to the house, but was still high in the woods above it.

Then he saw something white ahead and was not really surprised to find Laela seated on the trunk of a fallen tree.

She was obviously deep in thought.

When he could see her clearly, he noticed her head was thrown back and she was looking up at the trees overhead.

Her profile was silhouetted against them.

Her hands were clasped in her lap and he liked the serenity of her.

Then she heard *Victory's* hoofs and turned to look at who was approaching.

When she saw who it was she gave a little cry of delight.

The Marquis drew up beside her and she exclaimed:

"I thought you had . . . gone to the . . . Races!"

"That is where I thought you had gone," he replied.

She looked away from him a little shyly.

He knew perceptively there was some particular reason why she had stayed behind.

He dismounted, knotted *Victory's* reins on his neck, and left him loose.

He was taking a risk.

However, when he first inspected *Victory* after he arrived, Wainwright had told him the history of the stallion.

He had been taught by his previous owner, who had brought him up since he was a foal, to obey a whistle.

"I've tried it myself," Wainwright had said, "and it's true. *Victory* may be difficult in many ways, but he comes like a dog when he's called!"

As there was nothing handy to which the horse could be tied, the Marquis took a chance.

At the very worst, he could walk home.

Like most horses, *Victory* would return to the stable where he was well fed.

The Marquis sat down beside Laela on the tree-trunk.

He took off his hat and put it on the ground beside him.

"That is a magnificent horse you are riding!" she said.

"I have wanted to do so ever since I first saw him!" the Marquis answered. "And, as everybody except you has gone to the Races, I seized my opportunity."

"I am sure you enjoyed it," she said. "I have wanted to see you on a horse. I was sure you would ride as well as you drive."

"That is the sort of compliment I like to hear," the Marquis said as he smiled. "And from the way you speak, I imagine you too ride."

"Whenever I get the opportunity," Laela said, "and when Cousin Laurence was alive, he was very kind and always allowed me and Peter to ride any horse that was in his stables."

"Which I imagine you are not allowed to do since you moved in with Her Ladyship."

"That is true," Laela said in a low voice. "She makes sure I have . . . no time to do so by . . . keeping me . . . very busy."

"Is that why you could not go to the Races to-day?" the Marquis asked.

There was a little pause, and again Laela looked away from him as if she were embarrassed.

"I am waiting for an answer!" the Marquis said after a moment when she did not speak.

"You were so . . . wonderful last night to . . . save me," Laela said, "that I was . . . hoping there would be . . . a chance of . . . thanking you."

"And I was hoping for a chance," the Marquis replied, "to tell you that you were behaving very foolishly. Surely you know you should not have gone alone into the garden with a man like that?"

"I realised when . . . he tried to . . . kiss me that . . . I had been very . . . stupid," Laela said in a low voice, "but he just said, 'Let us go and look at the fountain!' I never dreamed . . . never thought he would . . . behave as he did."

"You are very young," the Marquis said, "but old enough to understand that you must never—and I repeat—*never*, accept an invitation to go alone with a man into the garden, the Conservatory, the Picture Gallery, or any other place, unless you want the man who suggests it to behave in the same manner."

The colour flooded into Laela's cheeks and she said:

"I . . . I am sorry I was so . . . foolish. If only . . . Mama were alive . . . she would . . . tell me about the things I should . . . and should . . . not do."

"I am sure your Mother, if she were alive, would not wish you to be staying where you are at the moment, with Sir Percy Crow," the Marquis said.

"I thought . . . that at dinner . . . and when that elderly man . . . suggested I should . . . go into the garden . . . I was . . . actually . . . escaping from . . . somebody else."

The words came jerkily from between her lips.

The Marquis knew she was embarrassed.

"Somebody else?" he asked. "What is his name?"

"I sat . . . next to him . . . at dinner," Laela replied, "and his name is . . . Mr. Denton-Parker."

The Marquis knew it was a name he had never heard before, and he asked:

"Tell me about him. Why did he upset you?"

"He . . . paid me . . . compliments," Laela said, "and they made me . . . feel uncomfortable because . . . he was being too . . . familiar."

The Marquis thought that, because Laela was so young, she would find the compliments the other women enjoyed made her shy.

"What do you know about this man?"

"He ... frightens ... me," Laela said. "He was ... waiting for me when I ... went back ... into the house ... and he insisted that I dance ... with him again ... I wanted to ... go to bed ... but it was impossible ... without seeming rude ... and then—"

She paused.

"And then ... ?" the Marquis prompted.

"He talked to ... Cousin Averil and ... complained that I was being ... unkind to him."

She made a little sound that was almost a sob as she went on:

"When it was time to go to bed, Cousin Averil came into my room and said I was being ridiculous. She lectured me about being 'difficult' and giving ... myself what she ... called 'airs.' "

"Why did she do that?" the Marquis enquired.

"Mr. Denton-Parker is very rich," Laela replied. "He made an enormous fortune during the War supplying the Army with boots and weapons."

The Marquis's lips tightened.

He knew all too well of the fortunes that had been made by men who stayed at home.

They were safe while others, like Charles and himself, fought and died.

"Go on," he said aloud. "What else did your Cousin say?"

"She said I ... would be very ... stupid if I did not ... accept all Mr. Denton-Parker had to ... offer me and that I could ... hardly expect her to ... keep me for ever!"

"And you would not think," the Marquis said slowly, "of accepting him because he is so rich?"

"There is . . . something about him which . . . makes my flesh creep . . . and . . . I do not . . . want his . . . money!"

The Marquis smiled.

"Then just be careful and try to avoid him until you leave here."

"That is . . . what I am . . . trying to do," Laela said, "and I managed it . . . to-day only by telling Cousin Averil I had not . . . finished the gown she . . . wants to wear for . . . dinner to-night."

She did not wait for the Marquis to say anything, but added:

"There is going to be . . . another Orchestra this evening . . . and I know I shall . . . not be able to . . . avoid Mr. Denton-Parker."

"Surely there is somebody in the party who is a decent sort of man," the Marquis asked, "who could talk to you, and who perhaps could help you keep Denton-Parker at a distance?"

He thought as he spoke the man's name that he was obviously like Sir Percy—a "social climber."

He would have added the hyphen to his name to make it sound more impressive.

"They all . . . seem to be very . . . much the same, but not quite as . . . bad as Mr. Denton-Parker," Laela said, "and they . . . drank a great deal of . . . wine at . . . dinner."

"There is only one answer," the Marquis said. "You must have a headache and go to bed early."

Laela smiled.

"Of course! That is what I will do! And I will tell Cousin Averil *before* dinner that I am not feeling well."

She looked up at the Marquis and said:

"How can I have . . . been so . . . stupid as not to think of that . . . myself?"

"What you have to realise," the Marquis said in a serious tone of voice, "is that you have been living very quietly in the Country with your Mother and Father and have not met many men. You have also become a very beautiful young woman, and that brings all sorts of difficulties in its wake."

He was well aware that Laela was staring at him in astonishment.

"Do you really mean," she asked in a tone of voice that sounded incredulous, "that I am pretty?"

"I said 'beautiful,' and I meant 'beautiful'! " the Marquis affirmed. "The two words are very different."

Laela gave a deep sigh.

"Mama was so beautiful that I used to pray every night I would grow up to . . . look just a . . . little bit . . . like her."

"Then your prayers have been answered," the Marquis said, "but I have to warn you that you must be very careful because men—all sorts of men, including those like Parker and the one I threw into the fountain—will find you irresistible."

"Both of them . . . are horrible . . . absolutely . . . horrible!" Laela said. "And perhaps it . . . would be . . . better if I looked ugly, or perhaps I should wear a . . . mask."

The Marquis laughed.

"It would certainly cause a great deal of comment, and make every man so curious that he would insist on trying to remove it."

"Now you are . . . frightening me," Laela said, "and please . . . do not let us go on talking about me . . . you have solved my problem . . . and I will go to bed with a headache immediately . . . after dinner. When I have finished saying my prayers and thanking God because . . . you are so clever . . . I will read a book."

"That is something I am afraid you will have to do a great number of times," the Marquis said, "if you continue to live with that rather flashy, over-dressed and under-bred Cousin of yours!"

Laela stared at him.

"Do you mean to . . . say you do not . . . admire Cousin Averil?"

"If you want the truth, I think she is vulgar and over-dressed!"

"That is . . . what I thought myself," Laela said in a low voice, "but . . . I was afraid you would . . . think I was being . . . unkind."

"It is not unkind to be discriminating," the Marquis said, "and that is why, Laela, you must not judge the men you meet in this house by those you would meet in London."

He paused and then continued:

"And I imagine from the lady's-maids I have met here that their mistresses are all rather in the same image as Lady Horncliffe."

"They are all very painted," Laela said in a low voice, "and I thought last night that Mama would not have . . . approved of the way . . . they talk or the way they . . . behave."

There was silence. Then she said:

"You . . . have not . . . changed your mind . . . about the cottage you said I could . . . rent?"

"No, of course not," the Marquis replied, "and as soon as your Cousin returns to London, which I imagine will be in another week or so, I will see that it is ready for you."

"I wish there were another word for 'thank you,' " Laela said, "and I am working with every moment I have so that when Peter and I arrive at the cottage I shall have . . . something . . . to sell."

"If you give me what you have finished before we reach London," the Marquis said, "I will sell it for you so that you will have some money, at least, to buy food."

Laela gave a deep sigh.

"Now you are being kind again, and as soon as I can . . . possibly do so I will pay you a . . . sensible rent for the cottage."

"There is no hurry," the Marquis said firmly, "and I have wondered why in fact you have absolutely nothing."

"I did have . . . five pounds," Laela said, "when Cousin Averil told me to come to her house and sew for her, but I gave it all to Miss Dean, the Governess who is looking after Peter. She has only a very small Pension to live on, and could not afford to keep him."

She looked at the Marquis a little nervously, as if she were afraid he would think her extravagant.

Then she said:

"Peter is big for his age . . . and he . . . always seems to . . . be hungry."

The Marquis thought of how apparently Lady Horncliffe resented anyone who ate what she considered too much.

He could understand why Laela was nervous of Peter having to live in such circumstances.

"I am quite sure," he said firmly, "I can get a good price for your handkerchiefs and anything else you make, and when we return to London I will get you orders for nightgowns and other things which women

106

consider essential to enhance their beauty!"

He thought with a little twist of his lips how many bills he had paid for such frivolities and how very expensive they were.

"I will work and work!" Laela promised. "But the difficulty at the moment is . . . getting the . . . materials."

"Then perhaps you would allow me to be your Banker?" the Marquis offered.

As he spoke, he remembered how often he had said those words.

It was something, he told himself, that he might have expected even of Laela.

Then he realised that she was looking at him with a shocked expression in her eyes.

"Of course I do not mean . . . that!" she exclaimed. "How can you think . . . when you have been so . . . kind and . . . wonderful to me that I could . . . expect you to . . . give me any of your . . . hard-earned money? Thank you . . . thank you for thinking of it, but it is . . . something I would never do . . . never, never!"

She spoke so determinedly that the Marquis asked:

"Why should it worry you?"

"Because you have to . . . earn your own . . . living," Laela said, "and I doubt if Cousin Averil is very . . . generous when it comes to . . . your wages."

She put out her hand to lay it on his arm.

"Please forgive me," she said, "for burdening you with my troubles when I am sure you have a lot of your own."

"Why should you think that?" the Marquis asked.

He thought she was choosing her words, until at last she said:

"I do not wish to sound as if I am . . . prying into your private affairs . . . but I am not foolish as to be unaware that you are a gentleman . . . so I know you must be . . . very, very poor to take . . . a job as . . . a coachman."

"Actually," the Marquis replied, "it is a job I rather enjoy. I like being with horses, and I like driving. If I have to work, at least I am out in the open air."

"At the same time . . . because you are so clever . . . there must be other things you can do. I shall pray very hard that you will find . . . something where you can be with your . . . friends and men who are like . . . yourself."

"I think you should be praying for yourself," the Marquis said, "and we both know that your Mother would not approve of the people with whom you are associating at the moment. Having seen them with your Cousin Averil, I think the sooner you move into the cottage I have offered you, the better!"

As he spoke, he was actually thinking that perhaps he could persuade one of his relatives to look after Laela and her small brother.

He knew as he thought about it that Peter was a liability.

He was sure his Grandmother, or one of his elderly Aunts, would welcome Laela as a companion.

It was quite another thing to expect them to take on a young boy.

'I will think of something,' he told himself confidently. 'In the meantime, the sooner Laela is away from Sir Percy Crow's house-party, the less likely she is to run into any more trouble than she has encountered already.'

"Let us take our fences one by one," he said aloud. "You must encourage your Cousin to leave here as soon as possible, and to look at the house she is thinking of buying in Herefordshire."

He paused and then continued:

"It will take us perhaps two days to get there, and after that she will return to London."

"That was the original plan," Laela replied, "but Cousin Averil is enjoying being here at Crowstock Towers because there are so many men to flirt with her and tell her how attractive she is."

"Then, I can see," the Marquis said with a sigh, "that you will have to suffer from a permanent headache in the evenings, and as you will be sitting upstairs doing nothing, you will have to allow me to buy you the muslin, linen, or any other sort of material you require."

Laela thought for a moment. Then she asked:

"Are you quite . . . quite sure . . . you can . . . afford it? You will not be . . . depriving yourself of . . . anything you would otherwise . . . enjoy?"

"I promise you I can afford it," the Marquis said, "and actually, as I told the rest of the staff, I had a win at Epsom before we left London and therefore could afford to give them the food to which they are entitled rather than the cheap meal with which Her Ladyship provided for them."

"You did that?" Laela exclaimed. "Oh, how kind of you! I am sure they were . . . very grateful!"

"Like you, they thanked me most profusely," the Marquis said, "but we are not concerned for the moment with anything but you, and I am sure I can find the type of material you want, and will do so at the next Town we pass on our way to Hereford."

She looked at him, and her eyes seemed to be filled with sunshine.

The Marquis rose to his feet.

"I must take *Victory* home," he said, "otherwise I am quite certain the Head Groom will think I have absconded with him."

Laela gave a little cry.

"You must not let him think . . . that! And please . . . do not do anything that would . . . annoy Cousin Averil . . . so that she would . . . dismiss you."

The Marquis thought she was very unlikely to do that. But he said aloud:

"Would it worry you if I had to leave and return to London in disgrace?"

"Oh, please," Laela said, "I could not . . . bear it! When you . . . saved me last night I thought how very . . . very lucky I was and . . . how horrible and . . . degrading it would have been if that . . . man had . . . kissed me as he was . . . trying to do."

"I was glad to be of service," the Marquis said a little mockingly.

"You are so . . . strong and I know of no other man who would have been able to pick him up so easily and throw him into the fountain!"

"I hope he leaves you alone in the future," the Marquis said.

"I think he will do that," Laela answered. "He avoided me at breakfast, and I expect he feels rather sheepish at being treated in such a cavalier fashion."

"It is a pity you cannot warn Parker he will get the same treatment!" the Marquis said.

He was aware as he spoke that Laela shivered.

Then, as if she could not bear to think about him, she walked a little way through the trees.

They could see *Victory* in the distance, looking for grass amongst the undergrowth.

"Wait a minute," the Marquis said, "I have an experiment to make."

Laela stopped and turned round to look at him.

He whistled, and for a moment thought *Victory* would pay no attention.

Then the horse lifted up his head and the Marquis whistled again.

Obediently the horse came trotting towards him.

Laela clapped her hands.

"How did you know he would come when you called him?" she asked.

"He has been trained to do since he was a foal," the Marquis answered, "but I was rather anxious in case the trick did not come off and I had to walk home."

Laela laughed, and it was a very pretty sound.

"If only you owned *Victory*," she said, "perhaps you would be able to perform in a Circus and the audience would applaud when he obeyed you."

"Do you think that would improve my position in life?" the Marquis asked. "I wonder if a Circus Performer rates higher than a coachman!"

He was speaking mockingly, but Laela thought seriously for a moment.

Then, as the Marquis was untying *Victory's* rein, she said:

"I think you would do well . . . at anything you . . . undertook, and it is just a question of your finding the place that suits you. Whatever your position was, you would undoubtedly do it . . . brilliantly and at the same time be . . . a personality."

"Thank you!" the Marquis said. "I have seldom received more encouraging appreciation of my talents!"

"I . . . I could say a lot more," Laela said, "but it . . . might make . . . you blush!"

111

"I think I am past blushing," the Marquis smiled. "At the same time, I shall look forward to hearing what else you think about me the next time we meet."

Laela was silent for a moment.

Then she said in a small, child-like voice:

"You . . . will try and . . . talk to me . . . again if there is any . . . chance of us . . . being . . . alone?"

"You know I will," the Marquis replied. "In the meantime, take care of yourself. And do not be alone with *any* man, even if he is blind and on crutches!"

Laela laughed as he meant her to do.

He swung himself into the saddle and, raising his hat, rode off through the wood.

Laela watched him go.

When he had vanished from her sight she gave a little sigh.

Then she started to walk down a path that she knew would lead her into the garden.

"He is wonderful! Absolutely wonderful!" she told herself. "How could I have been so fortunate as to find somebody so kind and so understanding?"

She looked up at the sky as she went on:

"I am sure, Mama, it is wrong of me to take the cottage without paying for it, and perhaps even worse to allow him to buy me materials. But I cannot think of any other way to make money."

She paused before she went on:

"I do not like to tell him that Cousin Averil has sold nearly all the things that were in our house."

She walked on until the house was in sight.

Then she stopped.

She was thinking how much she disliked the people in the house-party.

The men, who seemed to be drinking all the time, were noisy and familiar in a way she could not describe.

She just knew it was wrong.

The women, who were all older than she was, ignored her but made a tremendous fuss over her Cousin Averil.

She knew it was un-Christian, but she could not help knowing it was because she was so rich.

The things they said to her did not sound admiring, but envious.

Laela had thought last night and again this morning that the men were not gentlemen like her Father and Sir Laurence.

In fact, it was true what she had told Mr. Lyon, that he was a gentleman.

Mr. Denton-Parker, and Sir Percy, for that matter, were undoubtedly what her father would have described as being "Bounders."

She drew nearer the house.

Now she knew that in a short time the whole noisy crowd would be coming back from the Races.

"Please . . . God . . . take care . . . of me," she whispered as she went in through one of the French windows. "They . . . frighten . . . me!"

chapter six

LAELA had only just reached her bed-room when she heard the carriages coming back from the Races.

She was in a room at the end of the First Floor.

She realised it was a concession for her to be amongst Sir Percy's most favoured guests.

She imagined the room had originally been intended for a bachelor.

There were sporting prints on the over-elaborate wall paper.

In fact, it could have been attractive if the carpet had not been so new and so violent in colour.

She was, however, glad there was a large window over-looking the front of the house.

It enabled her to sew in the sunlight.

Looking out now, she saw the first carriage arrive at the front-door.

The occupants of it were very noisy.

A coach followed with more men than women, and they were even noisier.

She was sure the men must have imbibed a great deal at the Race-Course.

Judging from the way they were behaving, they had obviously enjoyed themselves.

She was glad she had not gone with them.

It had been fascinating to find John Lyon in the wood and talk to him.

It would be impossible to find another man who was as kind and understanding as he was.

He had advised her what to do and protected her.

She thought despairingly of how different it would be when he was no longer there.

Then she told herself it was a great mistake to suggest that he should get another position.

She could only hope that he would be content to stay on indefinitely with her Cousin.

She knew, however, how much the servants in London and those in the country resented the way the mistress treated them.

"If I weren't so old," the Housekeeper who had been with Sir Laurence for years had said, "I'd pack me boxes immediately and leave, and that's a fact, Miss Laela!"

"You must not do that!" Laela had pleaded. "The house would not be the same without you."

If it was not the Housekeeper, it was the Butler or the housemaids who polished everything so lovingly.

Then they learnt that Lady Horncliffe did not think the place impressive enough for her.

Laela could remember the shock it had been to the whole village.

She could not bear to think of the terror and despair she felt when she learned her home had been sold.

She and Peter had nowhere to go and no money.

At first she had been very grateful that Cousin Averil had asked her to stay

But when she learned she could not have Peter with her and Lady Horncliffe suggested he should go into an Orphanage, she hated her.

Hatred was something completely alien to Laela.

There had always been love in her house when her Father had been alive.

Although, when her Father died, her Mother had mourned him despairingly, she had loved her two children.

They clung to her because she was everything that was stable and beautiful in their lives.

Now, Laela thought, she and Peter were on their own.

She would have been frantic at the thought of the future if it had not been for John Lyon.

She had lain awake for a long time last night.

She was planning how she could make money, first to look after Peter, and second to pay for his education, and third to pay John Lyon a proper rent for the cottage.

The cottage would have to be furnished, but she did have just a few things left of her own.

When Cousin Averil had told her that she had sold the house, she said in a lofty manner:

"As you are coming to me, you will not need to bring anything with you. I have therefore sold it furnished."

Laela had gone down on her knees to beg that she might be allowed to have some of the treasures which her Mother had loved.

She had known them ever since she had been born.

There was a pretty French *secrétaire* at which her Mother had always written her letters.

There was an inlaid table on which her Father had stood his chess-board.

There were pictures, each of which had some special memory because her Father had told her their history.

Finally she had been allowed to take a pick of a very few things from the house before the new owner took possession.

The Vicar, because he felt sorry for Laela, had stored them in one of his out-houses.

She had not, however, been allowed to take a bed or curtains.

They would have to wait for those until John Lyon sold the things she was going to make.

'It is going to be difficult, very difficult,' she thought, 'but anything will be better than being parted from Peter and having to live with Cousin Averil grudging every penny we cost her.'

"With God's help we will manage," she told herself quietly, and lifted her small chin as if to defy the world.

The third coach arrived and the first person to emerge from it was Mr. Denton-Parker.

As she saw him, Laela instinctively moved away from the window to hide herself behind the curtains.

It was unlikely he would look up and see her, but even the sight of him made her shudder.

She had not told John Lyon the things he had said to her.

She was ashamed that any man should speak in such an intimate and familiar manner, especially as she had known him such a short time.

It was not only what he said, but the way he looked at her.

There was an expression in his eyes which she knew instinctively was wrong and almost evil.

"I must avoid him to-night," she told herself, "but I

wish Cousin Averil would decide to move on!"

It was getting near to dinner-time.

She washed and changed into the simple gown she had made herself.

She had used material from one of her Mother's gowns which was out of date.

It would certainly, she thought, not compare with the gowns worn by the other ladies.

But while she was unaware of it, it was a suitable frame for her beauty.

Its very simplicity and the way it revealed her slim figure and tiny waist made Laela look like a young goddess.

She was, however, more concerned about the gown she had altered for her Cousin than anything she wore herself.

It had been a complicated job.

The gown had been made by a Bond Street Dressmaker, and was heavily embroidered with *diamanté*.

It was very tight over the breast.

Laela, however, had managed to let it out.

She only hoped that her Cousin would approve of what she had done.

She was determined not to go downstairs until the very last minute before dinner was served.

If she did, Mr. Denton-Parker would single her out as he had done last night.

He made her feel conspicuous as he towered over her.

He looked at her with an expression in his eyes which made her uncomfortable.

He also took every opportunity to touch her hand, her arm, or her shoulder.

There was a knock on the door.

When Laela opened it, her Cousin Averil's lady's-maid stood there.

" 'Er Ladyship wants t'see you," she said.

She spoke in the somewhat aggressive voice she invariably used to Laela.

She resented her being useful to her mistress.

"I've always done the things you're now doin'!" she had said unpleasantly to Laela soon after she arrived. "And I 'ad no complaints."

"I am sure you sew beautifully," Laela said disarmingly, "but I am afraid it is my only talent. So I am very grateful to Her Ladyship for letting me work for her."

She often thought the lady's-maid, who was called Smithers, was in a better position than she was.

Smithers was paid very fairly, but she received no wages.

She had hoped that she would be given some money.

But soon after she had arrived, Lady Horncliffe had said:

"As I am keeping you and you are a companion and not a servant, there is no reason for you to need remuneration. You can ask me for anything you feel you have to buy."

Laela had been astounded seeing how many hours of sewing she had done.

Rather timidly, because she was nervous, she had said:

"I would like to have a little money of my own to be able to buy presents for Peter and . . . of course . . . you."

She added the last words as an after-thought, but Lady Horncliffe was not impressed.

"The presents you can give me are loyalty and gratitude," she said. "They are incalculable in terms of hard cash."

A few weeks later they were about to leave on the journey to Herefordshire.

Laela had dared to say shyly that she was in need of a shawl or a light coat.

"I am sure I can . . . buy one very cheaply," she said apologetically.

"I doubt it," Lady Horncliffe replied, "and I am sure I can find you something for which I no longer have any use."

After a long consultation with her lady's-maid she presented Laela with a coat that was worn and the colour faded.

Then she produced a gown that had a stain where a glass of claret had been spilt on it.

Lastly, there was a shawl that was so old it had lost several of its tassels.

Laela, by altering the gown, because she was smaller than her Cousin, had managed to conceal the mark on it.

She hoped the weather would be too warm to need a coat as she disliked the one her Cousin gave her.

The shawl made her feel like a "charity child."

Now, as if Smithers resented it, she said:

" 'Er Ladyship wants to see the gown you're altering, and if it ain't right, there'll be hell to pay!"

"I will come now," Laela replied.

She picked up her handkerchief and took a last glance in the mirror to see that her hair was tidy.

Then she hurried along the passage.

Lady Horncliffe was in one of the best Staterooms which had a huge four-poster bed and elaborately draped curtains.

There was furniture which was not particularly attractive, but which screamed "money."

The same applied to the carpet and the bed-spread.

Averil Horncliffe, who was wearing the most expensive under-clothes inset with lace, was waiting impatiently.

As Laela entered the room she complained:

"How can you take so long? I thought you had better help me into the gown, as you altered it."

"Yes, of course, Cousin Averil," Laela replied. "I do hope now you will find it comfortable."

"I shall be very annoyed it I don't!" Her Ladyship replied. "It cost me a pretty penny!"

Laela and Smithers put Lady Horncliffe into the gown.

Laela was greatly relieved to find that it fastened comfortably and she could find nothing to complain about.

She looked at herself in the mirror.

The *diamanté* on her corsage glittered in the light of the setting sun.

After a moment she announced:

"I will wear my diamond necklace."

"I thinks Your Ladyship'd chosen the turquoise one for to-night," Smithers exclaimed.

"I have changed my mind," Lady Horncliffe said. "And I will have the diamond earrings, the diamond bracelet, and, of course, my largest ring."

"They're all downstairs in the safe where Your Ladyship told me to put them!" Smithers said.

"Then go and fetch them—what are you waiting for?" Her Ladyship replied sharply.

Smithers went from the room, and when she had gone, Lady Horncliffe said:

"Now that we are alone, Laela, it gives me a chance to talk to you."

"What . . . about?" Laela asked a little nervously.

"Your ardent admirer—who else?"

Laela stiffened and Lady Horncliffe went on:

"He talked to me at the Races, and I think you are a very lucky girl!"

Laela did not speak and Lady Horncliffe continued:

"He told me that because he is so infatuated with you, he will not only give you a house in London with the Deeds in your name, but also he will put ten-thousand pounds in the Bank!"

Lady Horncliffe spoke in a voice of triumph.

Then she made a sweeping gesture with her hand.

"No-one could ask for better than that, and all I can say is that you had better accept it before he changes his mind!"

Laela drew in her breath.

She wanted to expostulate that she hated Mr. Denton-Parker and would not marry him if he were the last man on earth.

Then she knew that such a statement would only make her Cousin rage at her.

It would be much better to say what she felt to the man himself.

"He is so rich," Lady Horncliffe enthused, "that he even makes Sir Percy envious, and that, I can tell you, is saying something!"

She did not seem surprised that Laela said nothing, and went on:

"What a woman needs in this world is position and money, and I can assure you it is difficult to find both!"

She smiled at her reflection as she said:

"I have been fortunate, I admit that, and I intend to

conquer London, to be acclaimed by all the right people before I take another husband."

She gave a little giggle before she said:

"They keep asking me if I will let them put another wedding-ring on my finger, but I intend to see their bank balance before I give any of them an answer!"

She patted her hair into place before she said:

"Now, you be a sensible girl and tell Denton-Parker to-night that you will do what he wants, and leave all the arrangements in his hands."

She paused, then said:

"And by the way, I should not say a word about that tiresome little brother of yours until the ten-thousand pounds and the Deeds of the house are in your hands. That is my advice, and you will be a fool if you do not listen to me!"

There was fortunately no chance for Laela to reply.

The door opened and Smithers came back with her arms full of jewel-boxes.

By the time Lady Horncliffe was adorned and looked like a Christmas-tree, it was time to go downstairs.

As they entered the Drawing-Room, where everybody was to congregate before dinner, Laela saw Mr. Denton-Parker look first at Lady Horncliffe and then at her.

He knew she had been told of his generous offer.

She thought from the expression in his eyes that he was quite certain it would not be refused.

"I hate him! I hate him!" she said to herself.

Then, to her relief, Sir Percy was introducing her to some new guests who had arrived for dinner.

Because there was quite a number of them, they were interspersed between the members of the house-party at the dinner-table.

Laela found herself with a young man on either side of her.

She thought they differed in every way from Sir Percy's other friends.

Both men were interested in horses.

The conversation was therefore easy and by no means intimate.

They both looked in surprise, Laela thought, at the members of the house-party.

By the end of dinner they were drunk and excessively noisy.

"I will slip upstairs the minute the ladies leave the Dining-Room," Laela decided.

She only hoped her Cousin would not be aware that she had gone.

That made her think that she must wait until the dancing started and the gentlemen joined the ladies.

It was not as difficult as she feared.

When they reached the Drawing-Room, other guests from neighbouring houses, some of whom had been there the night before, were waiting.

There were drinks waiting for them on a large table.

It had been erected while they had been at dinner.

There was no reason, therefore, for the gentlemen to join Sir Percy in the Dining-Room.

It seemed to Laela that her Cousin took it upon herself to act as hostess.

She was soon surrounded by men toasting her and paying her compliments.

Laela knew this was her chance to escape.

She slipped out of the room and was only just in time.

As she did so, she saw at the end of the passage Sir Percy coming from the Dining-Room.

She ran up the stairs into her bed-room.

Only when she had shut the door behind her did she feel safe.

"If only I could talk to John Lyon," she said, "he would tell me what to do."

Both Mr. Denton-Parker and her Cousin Averil were pressing her to say "Yes."

It was going to be very difficult to defy them.

*　*　*

Supper in the Housekeeper's room was late that evening because of the large number of people arriving from outside.

Finally, when the Butler was free, they sat down in the same precedence as before.

"Two Balls two nights runnin's too much of a good thing if you asks me!" the Housekeeper said to the Marquis.

"It is certainly very hard on the staff," he agreed.

"My girls didn't finish clearin' up everything 'til two o'clock in th' morning," the Housekeeper said, "and it'll be dawn afore we finishes to-night!"

"It is very hard on you, too," the Marquis said sympathetically.

"You understand, Mr. Lyon," the Housekeeper enthused, "and t'was very different when His Lordship were here."

"I expect you miss him," the Marquis remarked.

"More than I like to say," the Housekeeper replied. "Sir Percy's generous, I can't say he's not, but it's not like t'were in t'old days."

She sighed.

The Marquis knew she could say a great deal more if she wished to.

There was the usual gossip round the table in which he took no part.

It had been quite amusing the first night to know that upstairs, or downstairs, no one could resist to blacken up some wretched woman's character.

It also confirmed what he had always believed—that no gentleman was a hero to his Valet.

Now he longed to have a long talk with Lord Charles and be drinking at White's with men of his own class.

At last the long-drawn-out supper ended.

The Marquis said good-night, saying he wanted to walk in the garden before it was filled with loving couples from the Ball-Room.

"Now, you be careful what you does, Mr. Lyon," one of the lady's-maids said. "I hear poor Mr. Mortimer was chucked in the fountain by one of them rowdy young Bucks last night. Wringing wet he was!"

"And a nice mess his clothes was in!" Mr. Mortimer's Valet exclaimed. "I spent hours this mornin' putting 'em back to rights."

"I will certainly be careful," the Marquis said as he walked towards the door.

He hoped as he moved along the passage that Laela was obeying his instructions.

If she did, she would not go into the garden with anyone, however hard they pressed her to do so.

He could hear a lot of noise coming from the Dining-Room.

He was aware that long before the ladies had left, the gentlemen must have been what was called "foxed."

Or, as they would have expressed it, "drunk as a Lord."

'Thank God drunkenness is not one of my vices!' he thought.

In fact, he was very abstemious because he wished to keep down his weight so that he rode light.

Anyway, he always thought that any man who drank too much made a fool of himself.

He was passing the Pantry and saw there were a number of men-servants congregated there.

He would have gone on without noticing them when he heard one of them say:

"I'll be promised two guineas from 'Mr. Bags-o' Gold'!"

"D'you mean Mr. Denton-Parker?" another asked.

"That's 'im, an' wot d'you think 'e wanted?"

The Marquis, moving down the passage, was not really listening.

Then, just before he was out of ear-shot, he heard the answer.

"The key of 'er bed-room, that's wot!"

The Marquis stopped dead.

It flashed through his mind that the one thing he had not told Laela to do was to lock her bed-room door.

Now, if he had heard right, it would be impossible for her to do so.

He walked slowly back.

He could see quite clearly the young footman who had been talking holding up a key.

"Ye should 'ave asked more," one of the other footmen was saying. " 'Er be a pretty piece, an' 'e be made o' money!"

"Two guineas ain't too bad!" the footman holding the key said defensively.

The Marquis stood in the shadows, wondering what he should do.

Finally he made up his mind and said casually:

"You'd better look out! We have finished in Mrs. Field's room."

The footmen started at the sound of his voice and realised he was warning them.

If supper was over in the Housekeeper's room, it meant that the Butler would soon be along.

There would be trouble if they were not in their right places.

The footmen who were supposed to be on duty in the hall scurried off.

Those who had been waiting on the guests in the Dining-Room turned to the sink to wash the silver *entrée* dishes.

The footman with the key was about to follow the others, when the Marquis caught hold of him.

"I will give you three sovereigns for that key!"

"Mr. Denton-Parker said I were t'get it for 'im!"

"I know that," the Marquis replied, "but I have made you a better offer, and you must make your choice."

The footman drew the key from his pocket.

" 'Ow about four sovereigns," he asked, "an' I'll say there were't one there."

The Marquis took four sovereigns from his pocket.

"You drive a hard bargain," he said, "and will doubtless go far in the world—like your Master!"

He spoke sarcastically.

But the footman merely took the sovereigns from his hand and thrust them into his pocket.

"You're a sport," he said, "an' I 'opes as you enjoys yerself!"

The Marquis felt like punching him for his impudence.

"If you talk about this," he said, "I will knock your head off!"

He spoke in his low, menacing voice which had frightened much stronger men.

"I wouldn't do nothin' like that, Mr. Lyon," the footman said quickly. "I swear!"

"You had better not!" the Marquis said ominously.

He walked up the stairs.

When he reached the First Floor he saw one of the housemaids coming out of the Stateroom.

" 'Allo, Mr. Lyon," she said. "What are you doin' up 'ere?"

"I have a message from Her Ladyship for Miss Horn," he replied. "Be an angel, and tell me which is her room."

"I'm always ready t'be an angel with the likes of you," the housemaid giggled.

She was getting on for forty, but she managed to look coy.

"I can see your wings sprouting!" the Marquis replied, and she giggled again.

"Missy be right at the end—last door," she said, pointing. "She's there 'cause I sees 'er come up some time ago."

"You should wear your halo the next time I see you!" the Marquis said.

He heard her laugh as she walked away.

He reached Laela's door and knocked on it gently.

There was a little pause before she said:

"Come in!"

He opened the door, and Laela looked up in surprise.

Her silver-gold hair was falling over her shoulders.

She was wearing a pretty dressing-gown that buttoned up to the neck.

It made her look very young and child-like.

She was seated at a table on which there were three candles.

She was sewing Lady Horncliffe's gown which had been torn last night when she was dancing.

The Marquis came into the room.

Then, because she had never imagined he would come to her bed-room, she asked:

"What is . . . the matter . . . what has . . . happened?"

He shut the door behind him.

"This!" he said, taking the key from his pocket.

Laela put down her sewing and rose from the table.

"What is it?" she asked.

"It is the key to your door!"

She drew in her breath.

"How did you . . . get it? Who had . . . taken it . . . away?"

"That is the whole point," the Marquis said. "Surely you realise that in a house like this you should have locked your door?"

Laela's eyes widened.

"I . . . I never . . . thought of . . . it!"

"It is something you must think about in the future, Laela!" the Marquis said severely.

"But . . . I . . . do . . . not understand . . . !"

"Denton-Parker offered one of the footmen two guineas if he would bring this key to him!"

Laela's face went pale.

"Mr. Denton-Parker?" she whispered. "Do you . . . mean . . . ?"

"I mean he intended calling on you later this evening!"

"Oh, no! How . . . could he . . . think of anything . . . so . . . terrible!"

"It would have been quite easy for him to do so,"

the Marquis said, "if you had not been able to lock your door, but apparently the idea had not occurred to you."

"Of course . . . it had . . . not! How could . . . I have . . . imagined . . . how could . . . I have thought that . . . any man would . . . do anything . . . like that?"

"Think of it now," the Marquis said, "and in future be very, very careful to lock yourself in. If the key has disappeared as this one had done, go at once to the Housekeeper and ask for another room."

Laela clasped her hands together.

"How could any man . . . behave in such a . . . despicable . . . manner? And he . . . made Cousin Averil . . . tell me . . . what he is . . . prepared to . . . offer me . . . and she is . . . pressing . . . me to . . . accept."

Laela's words were falling over each other and were almost incoherent.

"Offer you? What has he offered you?"

"A house . . . with the . . . Deeds in my . . . name . . . and ten-thousand pounds . . . in the . . . Bank!"

"Quite generous!" the Marquis said sarcastically. "However, at your age, I should imagine you would want a wedding-ring."

He saw, as he spoke, the puzzled expression in Laela's eyes.

"He is asking . . . me to marry . . . him," she said.

"He is married already!" the Marquis answered. "I was speaking about him to his Valet this evening, and he told me he has been married for ten years and has three children!"

Laela put her hands up to either side of her face.

"Do . . . you mean . . . that? But . . . Cousin Averil said . . . oh . . . how . . . could she? How could she . . .

think I would . . . do anything so . . . wrong . . . so wicked!"

"You had no idea he was offering you a position as his mistress?" the Marquis asked.

"No! No! I . . . never thought that . . . a gentleman would . . . suggest . . . such a . . . thing so—"

Her voice broke.

"He is . . . evil . . . I knew he was . . . evil! And now . . ."

"Now," the Marquis said firmly, "you will lock yourself in and to-morrow I hope you will tell Mr. Denton-Parker exactly what you think of him."

He knew as he spoke there was a stricken expression in Laela's eyes.

She was shocked in a way he had never seen a woman be before.

He put the key into the lock.

He was just about to open the door, when he heard footsteps outside.

He knew it would be a mistake to be seen leaving her room.

He put his finger to his lips in case she should speak.

At the same time, he turned the key in the lock.

There was a knock on the door, and both the Marquis and Laela stiffened.

She did not move, and after a moment the knock came again.

The Marquis looked at Laela and nodded.

In a faint, frightened voice she asked:

"W-who . . . is it?"

It was then that whoever was outside tried to open the door.

As it was locked, it was impossible to open, then came Denton-Parker's voice, saying:

"Laela, open the door! I have something important to tell you!"

Laela moved towards the Marquis as if for protection.

When she was close to him she said:

"It is . . . too late . . . I am going to . . . sleep."

"I will not keep you long," Denton-Parker replied. "I have a message from your Cousin."

"What . . . is it?"

"I cannot tell you here, standing outside."

As he spoke he tried the door again and the Marquis thought he was swearing beneath his breath.

"I am . . . going to . . . sleep," Laela said, "tell . . . Cousin Averil I will . . . come and . . . see her first . . . thing in the morning."

"I want to see you now!" Denton-Parker replied.

Instinctively, the Marquis felt from the way he was speaking that he intended to try to burst the door open.

Quickly he turned round and put his shoulders against it.

He knew it would take a very strong man to move him.

He had, however, been right in his assumption.

Denton-Parker stood back, then flung himself violently against the door.

If the Marquis had not been there, he might have been able to burst it open.

Although the key jangled in the lock, the Marquis's large frame prevented the door from giving way.

Now, undoubtedly, Denton-Parker was swearing, and not beneath his breath.

He made one more attempt to break down the door, but it was a comparatively feeble effort.

There was silence. Then he went away.

The Marquis listened until there was no longer any sound of his footsteps.

Laela was listening too.

Now she gave a little cry which was like that of a small animal caught in a trap.

She flung herself against the Marquis.

"You . . . saved me . . . you . . . saved me!" she cried. "How could . . . you have . . . been here . . . at exactly the . . . right moment?"

She clung to him and he put his arms around her.

He realised as he did so that she was trembling all over.

Then she said in a voice of terror:

"He may . . . try again . . . what shall . . . I do . . . how shall I . . . escape? I must . . . go away!"

She looked up at the Marquis as she spoke.

There were tears in her eyes and her lips were quivering.

She was also still trembling with fear.

The Marquis thought that although she was frightened, he had never seen a woman look more lovely.

At the same time, she was very much in need of protection.

"It is all right," he said soothingly. "He will not try again to-night."

"But . . . what will . . . happen to-morrow . . . when Cousin Averil . . . tries to . . . make me . . . as . . . wicked as he is?"

Only now was she aware of the full implication of what had been intended.

"Tell . . . me . . . what I . . . can do . . . please . . . tell me!" she pleaded.

Without thinking, without considering anything but

that she was very lovely and in his arms, the Marquis kissed her.

His lips came down on hers and he held her close against him.

For a moment Laela was still from sheer astonishment.

Then, as the Marquis held her mouth captive, her whole body seemed to melt into his.

It was as if, she thought, he opened the Gates of Heaven and took her inside.

As he went on kissing her, she knew she had loved him from the first moment she had seen him.

Whether he wanted her or not, she belonged to him and was a part of him.

The Marquis's kiss seemed to have taken the stars from the sky and put them in her breast.

She felt as if the light of them shimmered through her.

It was the light that came from God and was everything that was beautiful and perfect.

Laela's lips awoke sensations within the Marquis that he had never experienced before.

He could hardly believe that what he was feeling was so different, or that he was not kissing just another woman, as he had kissed so many.

It was such a strange, rapturous sensation that swept over him that he could not explain it even to himself.

He knew without really thinking about it that the ecstasy Laela was feeling was also what she had aroused in him.

They were close in a manner that he had never known before in any of his many love-affairs.

After what seemed a century, or it might have been just a few minutes, he raised his head.

He saw that Laela's face was transformed into a beauty that had nothing human about it.

It was as if she were part of the Divine.

Gone were the tears, the fear, the shock, the horror she had expressed before he touched her.

Instead, she radiated a love which came not from her body but from her soul.

For a moment they just looked at each other.

Then, as if words were superfluous, the Marquis was kissing her until he felt they were floating in the sky and the world no longer contained them.

Again a century passed before he said, and it was difficult to recognise his own voice:

"My Darling! What have you done to me? How can you have made me feel like this?"

"I . . . I love . . . you!" Laela whispered. "But . . . I never thought . . . you would . . . want to . . . kiss me."

"I cannot think why I waited so long!" the Marquis replied, and kissed her again.

Later still, he said:

"You cannot stay in this house."

There was a little pause, as if Laela had difficulty in remembering where she was.

Then she said:

"You do . . . understand . . . I have . . . to . . . escape."

"Of course I do," the Marquis agreed. "Pack your things; we will leave at once!"

Her eyes widened.

"Leave?" she asked. "But . . . I must not . . . hurt you . . . or make you . . . lose your job."

The Marquis smiled.

"Are you really thinking of me?"

"Of course I . . . must think . . . of you," she said. "If you could . . . just tell me . . . where I can . . . go where that . . . man will not . . . find me . . ."

"I promise you he will not be able to do that. Now do as I said—pack your things."

He thought for a moment. Then he asked:

"Are you strong enough to carry your own box downstairs?"

"Yes . . . of course . . . I am."

"Then when you are dressed come to the stables. I will be waiting for you there, and it would be better if nobody in the house knows we have gone until the morning."

"What about . . . Cousin . . . Averil?"

"If she worries about you, it will serve her right!" he said. "She had no right to suggest—"

He was going to say more, but he thought it might upset Laela again.

Instead, he kissed her gently and said:

"Do as I tell you. Leave everything to me, and I promise you it will be all right."

Her eyes seemed to glow like stars.

Then she said in an anxious little voice:

"You are . . . quite certain . . . it will . . . not damage you in . . . any way. You will . . . never get a . . . reference . . . from Cousin Averil."

"I can manage quite well without it," the Marquis said. "Stop worrying about anything but making your escape."

He pulled her close against him and said in a voice that was one of dedication:

"I love you, Laela!"

He turned towards the door, and as he opened it he said:

"Lock the door while you are dressing—just in case!"

He saw the fear in Laela's eyes.

"I will . . . be very . . . very . . . quick!" she answered, and smiled at him.

Out in the passage he ran without pretending he was doing anything else to his own bed-room.

It took him only a few seconds to pack the small amount of things he had with him.

He also retrieved his money from where he had hidden it.

Then he went down the back stairs and out to the stables.

He was half-afraid that Wainwright would have gone to bed.

To his relief, however, he found him as usual reading the Sporting Papers in the Harness-Room.

"Hallo, Lyon!" he exclaimed as the Marquis appeared. "I wasn't expectin' yer."

"I hoped you would be here," the Marquis said.

He walked into the Harness-Room, where Wainwright had his paper open on a table, and put down two ten-pound notes.

"Those are for you if you will help me," he said.

He put five others of the same denomination in a separate pile and added:

"Those are a guarantee that I will send back what I intend to borrow from you."

Wainwright looked at him in surprise.

"What's that?" he asked.

"A Travelling Chariot and two horses, and I want your best!"

"An' you really think I'll let you have them?"

"I would like to think you trusted me, and I swear to you they will come back to you in the same condition as I take them. As you well know, it is very unlikely that Sir Percy will be aware they are missing."

There was a long silence, and the Marquis just looked at Wainwright.

He was using his will-power as he had in the War.

Finally Wainwright succumbed.

"All right, Lyon," he agreed. "I may be a fool, but I trust ye, and I'll be very surprised if you let me down."

"I promise I will not do that," the Marquis said. "I would give you a cheque to the full value of what I am borrowing, but the signature on it will not be 'Lyon.' But it would be best in case anything occurs for you to know as little as possible about me."

Unexpectedly Wainwright laughed.

"I allus knew there was some mystery 'bout you!" he said. "But as I 'spect you're in a hurry, there's no point in going on talking."

He picked up the notes which the Marquis had laid on the table and put them into his pocket.

Then he called in a loud voice for the grooms who were on duty.

By the time Laela arrived in the stable-yard, two of Sir Percy's finest bred horses were between the shafts of a Travelling Chariot.

It was light and had been purchased only three months before.

As soon as the Marquis saw Laela, he hurried to take her box from her.

He looked at her.

As she smiled up at him, he thought that no woman could look more lovely, or more happy.

"You are . . . really taking me . . . away?" she asked in a low voice.

"At once," he answered. "Everything is ready."

He helped her into the Chariot, which had two seats in front.

There was also one for a groom to sit behind them, but it was empty.

Because it was a warm night, the hood was down.

The Marquis knew the moon would light the way far more effectively than the two candle-lanterns which hung on the sides of the Chariot.

Having helped Laela into the carriage, he tucked a rug round her.

Then he went to the other side to climb into the driving-seat.

He held out his hand to Wainwright.

"Thank you," he said. "I will never forget your trust in me, and I will be writing to you in another capacity in the near future."

"Good Luck, and God bless you both!" Wainwright replied with a smile.

The Marquis took up the reins and they drove out of the yard and down the drive.

As they went out through the large, impressive gates and onto the road, Laela moved a little closer to him.

"I think . . . I must be . . . dreaming!" she said. "And I am . . . afraid I shall . . . wake up."

"We are both dreaming," the Marquis said, "and it is a dream come true!"

He knew as he spoke that it was the truth.

He had found something which he had thought he would never find and which would always elude him.

It was quite simply called "Love."

chapter seven

THE Marquis drove for about an hour-and-a-half.

He then thought, as the road was narrow and twisting, they had better rest for what was left of the night.

It was after one o'clock when he drove into a small village.

He remembered passing through it several times when he had been hunting.

It was very pretty with a black-and-white Inn on the village Green.

There was the inevitable duck-pond surrounded by kingcups.

As he drew up his horses, Laela asked:

"Why are we stopping?"

"Because I do not want you to be tired," the Marquis replied tenderly, "and we still have quite a long way to go to-morrow morning."

He handed her the reins and said:

"Hold the horses while I go inside and see what I can arrange."

He walked up to the Inn, which was closed.

Going round to the back, where he thought the Innkeeper would be sleeping, he managed to wake him.

"What d'you want . . ." he said truculently, until he saw the Marquis standing in the moonlight, and added, " . . . Sir?"

"I am sorry to disturb you," the Marquis said, "but I am with my sister, and it is difficult to go any farther, so we would like to stay with you for the night. I will make it worth your while."

The Innkeeper did not wait to hear any more, but flung on his clothes and hurried downstairs.

In the meantime, the Marquis looked over the stable.

There were two really clean stalls which could accommodate the horses.

He took the precaution of filling the pails with fresh water.

He was sure that Wainwright would have put a bag of oats at the back of the Chariot.

When he came from the stable, the Innkeeper was waiting for him.

"Oi be afraid, Sir," he said, "Oi 'ave only one Guest-Room, but there be a sofa in it."

"I will take it," the Marquis said, "and I have found I can put my horses into your stable."

When the Innkeeper came outside and saw the Chariot and the horses, he was clearly impressed.

The Marquis drove them into the stable-yard and the Innkeeper helped him to unharness them.

In the meantime, the Innkeeper's wife, realising what was happening, had taken Laela up to the Guest-Room.

It was a pleasant room with a beamed ceiling.

There were two windows, one of which overlooked the Green, the other the back of the Inn.

There was, however, only one large bed and a sofa.

"Oi 'ears the gent'man say 'e 'ad 'is sister with 'im," the Innkeeper's wife said to Laela, "an' Oi knows my 'usband explained it's the only room us've left. But yer brother can sleep on t'sofa, an' ye can take th' bed. Oi'll fetch some more blankets an' another pillow."

She brought these back and laid them on the sofa before she asked:

"Be there anythin' more ye'll be wantin', Miss?"

"No, thank you," Laela replied. "I am sure we will be very comfortable."

When the Innkeeper's wife had gone, she pushed the sofa as far as possible from the bed.

She then began to quickly undress.

By looking out through the window she could see the Marquis in the stable with the Innkeeper.

They had lit a lantern and she could see the top of the Marquis's head as he rubbed down one of the horses.

"He is so . . . wonderful!" she said to herself. "And thank . . . You . . . thank . . . You . . . God for . . . letting me . . . find him!"

When they had finished with the horses, the Innkeeper insisted that the Marquis have a drink.

As it happened, he was thirsty.

The large mug of cider the Innkeeper poured out for him was very welcome.

"I would like to take some up for my sister," he said. "We have come quite a long way."

"Oi wishes Oi 'ad somethin' else t'offer ye," the Innkeeper said, "but Oi dare say there's some ham for ye, if ye fancies it."

"We are not hungry," the Marquis answered, "but I enjoyed the cider and you can refill my mug."

The Innkeeper obliged.

The Marquis climbed up the wooden staircase carrying the two mugs of cider.

He managed to open the door of the bed-room.

There were two candles alight beside the bed, but the bed itself was empty.

Then he realised that Laela was on the other side of the room on the sofa.

He was just about to speak when in the light from the candle he could see that her eyes were closed.

She was fast asleep.

He put down the mugs by the side of the bed and walked across the room to look at her.

He knew of no other woman who would have taken the sofa rather than the bed, and, for that matter, not expected him to join her in it.

He knew it was an idea that would never had entered Laela's head.

He stood looking down at her fair, silvery hair falling on either side of her small face.

Her hand which lay outside the blanket was relaxed.

He thought that no-one could look so lovely and at the same time so innocent.

He wanted to go down on his knees to kiss her lips until she awoke.

He knew that to touch her would reawaken the inexpressible rapture which had carried them both into a Heaven of their own.

Yet he was well aware that Laela was tired, not only from the journey, but also from the drama of running away.

Besides this, there was the terror that Denton-Parker had aroused in her.

"I must let her sleep," the Marquis decided.

It did not occur to him that perhaps for the first time

in his life he was not thinking of himself but being completely and utterly unselfish.

Moving softly about the room, he undressed, extracted his nightshirt from his luggage, and got into bed.

Before he blew out the candle he took one last look at Laela across the room.

Once again he was thanking God he had found her.

* * *

Laela was dreaming that she was being kissed.

She felt as if the sunshine moved through her body.

The world was too golden to be real.

Then, as she opened her eyes, she realised that the Marquis was kissing her.

She put her arms around his neck to draw him closer.

He kissed her until she was fully awake.

Then he said:

"I would like to stay here kissing you all day, and telling you how lovely you are, but we have quite a long way to go."

She saw he was dressed, it was morning, and she said, still a little sleepily:

"I . . . I did not hear you . . . come to . . . bed."

"You were fast asleep, and it was very kind of you to take the sofa, which I should have done."

"No . . . of course not," she replied. "It would have been too small for you . . . but I meant to stay awake and make sure . . . you were . . . comfortable."

"Another time you must look after me!" he teased.

"That is what . . . I want . . . to do," Laela replied.

"I will go and get the horses ready," he said, "then we will have some breakfast before we leave."

She smiled at him, and he went from the room carrying his own box.

Laela jumped up quickly and ran to the window.

She could not resist watching the Marquis cross the yard towards the stable.

She thought no man could look smarter or more handsome.

"How can he possibly . . . love me?" she asked herself humbly.

By the time she was dressed, the Marquis had put the horses between the shafts.

He found a boy to hold them, and was waiting at a table in the Parlour which had been laid ready for breakfast.

Unlike the fashionable women in London, he noticed, Laela ate a large breakfast.

She enjoyed eggs and bacon and slices of new bread from a cottage loaf, spread with butter and honey.

The Marquis was aware that both the Innkeeper and his wife were curious about them.

He managed with some dexterity to evade answering any direct questions.

When he paid him for their lodgings for the night, the Innkeeper was so grateful at his generosity that he forgot everything else.

They drove off in the sunshine.

Only when they had gone quite a long way along the country lanes did Laela ask:

"Where are we . . . going?"

"To be married!" the Marquis said quietly.

She looked up at him, and he thought a thousand candles might have been lit behind her eyes.

"Do you . . . do you mean . . . that?" she asked in a whisper.

"I love you," the Marquis replied, "and I think you love me, so what else can we do?"

"I . . . I love you," Laela said, "I love you . . . until there is . . . nobody else in the . . . whole world but you. . . . At the same time—"

She hesitated a moment before she said:

"Can you really . . . afford to be married?"

Before he could answer, she went on:

"I will . . . work for you . . . of course I will . . . but I would not . . . want to be an . . . encumbrance . . . and you might . . . not find it easy to . . . get another job if you have . . . a wife."

"Then what do you suggest we do?" the Marquis asked.

He wanted to hear the answer and wondered what it would be.

"I . . . suppose . . . if we were . . . sensible," Laela replied, "we would wait . . . until you . . . find a job where they . . . would not . . . object to your having a . . . wife."

"But that would be very frustrating for both of us," the Marquis objected. "I want you with me now, at this moment, and for ever, Laela!"

"That is . . . what I want . . . too," she said, "but you have been so . . . kind and wonderful to me that . . . I could not bear you to . . . suffer on . . . my account."

"I think you can leave all those things to me," the Marquis said as he smiled, "if you are quite certain you do not mind being poor with me."

"Being *with* you . . . is the only thing . . . that matters," Laela answered, "and I will . . . scrub floors, beg in the streets, or do anything . . . so long as I can . . . be with you . . . and be . . . your . . . wife."

She spoke the last word very softly, as if it made her feel shy.

The Marquis thought that he had the answer for Charles.

He said that no-one would marry him for himself alone.

He was so happy that he had found Laela, he wanted to proclaim to the whole world that she was different from any other woman.

That she wanted him as a man, and not just because he was a wealthy Marquis.

But the only person who would ever know the true story would be Charles.

He had lost his bet but had found a wife.

He was, however, certain Charles would give him *Tempest* as a wedding present.

They drove on.

As the Marquis had reckoned, it was past midday when they turned in through the huge, impressive gold-tipped wrought-iron gates of Eagles.

He saw Laela glance at them in surprise.

Then, as they proceeded up the long drive with its ancient oak-trees, she was obviously entranced with the loveliness of it.

The Marquis knew exactly the place where he would stop to give her the best view of Eagles.

He pulled the horses to a standstill.

Laela could see ahead of them the great house which had been built by the Marquis's ancestor in the reign of Queen Elizabeth.

The sunlight was reflected on a hundred windows.

The statues and urns on the roof were silhouetted against the blue sky.

A green lawn sloped down to the oval-shaped lake which lay below the house.

As Laela gazed entranced, a flight of white doves

150

flew across the front of the house and settled in the garden.

A profusion of almond trees and magnolias were in bloom.

The Marquis waited.

"Could anything be . . . more beautiful?" Laela asked. "To whom does it belong?"

"To me!" the Marquis said.

Laela laughed.

"Mama and I always used to say exactly that whenever we saw anything lovely. We might not own it, but we could hold its beauty within our hearts and so it was ours—ours for ever and nobody could take it from us."

She spoke in a rapt little voice which the Marquis thought was moving.

He did not say anything, but drove on.

They crossed the bridge which spanned the lake.

As they climbed up towards the court-yard in front of the house, Laela said a little nervously:

"Perhaps . . . you ought . . . not to go . . . so close! People might . . . think we are . . . prying."

They reached the long flight of steps to the front-door.

Two footmen who had obviously been watching their approach ran out to set down the red carpet.

Almost as if by magic the Butler appeared in the doorway.

A groom came hurrying from the stables towards them.

Laela turned and looked enquiringly up at the Marquis.

"It is all right, my Darling," he said.

She stared at him in astonishment.

He went round the Chariot to help her out, and taking her hand, drew her up the steps.

As they reached the front-door the Butler said:

"Good-morning, M'Lord! It's nice to see Your Lordship, but we were not expecting you."

Because the Marquis was holding Laela's hand, he was aware of a sudden tightening of her fingers on his.

"We have come some distance, Mullins," the Marquis replied, "so I want luncheon as soon as possible—and tell Mrs. Meadows to prepare the Queen's Room for Miss Horn."

"The Queen's Room, M'Lord?"

"That is what I said," the Marquis answered, "and send a groom with a carriage to tell the Vicar I wish him to be here at two o'clock."

"Very good, M'Lord."

It was obvious that Mullins was astonished at what had been said.

At the same time, he was too well-trained to comment.

The Marquis led Laela into the room he always used when he was alone at Eagles.

It contained the desk at which he wrote.

He kept the books there which he most enjoyed reading, although there were ten-thousand volumes in the great Library.

There were a number of sporting prints on the walls.

There was also a portrait of his Mother which hung over the mantelpiece.

She was wearing her Peeress's robes, the Mounteagle diamond tiara, and looked very beautiful.

As the door closed behind the Butler, Laela turned to look at the Marquis.

In a small, frightened little voice she said:

"I . . . I do not . . . understand. Why are . . . we . . . here? And . . . why did he . . . call you . . . 'My Lord'?"

"I am afraid I have been deceiving you, my precious," the Marquis replied. "I am actually the Marquis of Mounteagle, and this is my home."

For a moment Laela was very still, almost as if she had turned to stone.

To his surprise, she gave a little cry of anguish.

"No . . . no! It . . . cannot be . . . true!"

She moved away to stand at the window with her back to him, and he knew she was crying.

He walked up to her and, putting his arms around her, he pulled her tenderly against him.

"Why are you crying?" he asked. "Does it matter that I am not a poor Coachman?"

"I . . . I thought . . . I was to be . . . your . . . w-wife," Laela stammered.

"That is exactly what you will be," he replied. "We will be married when the Vicar arrives at two o'clock."

"No, no . . . of course . . . not."

He could hardly hear the words, and yet they were said.

"Why do you say that?" he asked.

"Because if . . . you are so . . . grand . . . and live in this . . . great house . . . you cannot marry . . . somebody like . . . me."

"Why not?" the Marquis asked.

"Because you must . . . marry a woman as . . . grand and . . . important as . . . yourself."

"No-one can be more important to me than you are," the Marquis said, "and as the Marchioness of Mounteagle, you will be very grand."

She shook her head, then hid her face against his shoulder.

The Marquis kissed her hair.

He had always believed that any woman to whom he proposed marriage would be thrilled and excited by the idea.

Fleur had pretended to be, while all the time she was hoping for a better offer.

But he had never thought anyone would refuse him.

"I want to ask you something, Laela," he said, "and it is very important that you answer me truthfully."

"You . . . know I will . . . do that," she murmured.

"Did you really mean it when you said that if we were married you would work so that we would be comfortable, even if you had to scrub floors?"

"Of course . . . I would do . . . anything if it . . . meant that I could make . . . you happy."

"It will make me very happy if you were here, and I am asking you to help me with all the many things I have to do."

"But . . . there are . . . so many other . . . women who could do that much . . . better than . . . I could."

"That is for me to decide," the Marquis said, "and I know, my darling, that you will inspire me and, I am afraid, keep me working when all I want is to make love to you."

Laela made a little sound that was half a laugh.

"I thought you loved me!" he said.

"I do! I do love you . . . oh . . . I do! But I am . . . thinking of you."

"Then if you love me, you have to marry me, for I could not be happy without you."

She raised her eyes to his, and her eyes searched his face.

"Is that ... really true? Do you ... swear it on ... everything ... you hold ... sacred?"

"I swear it!" the Marquis said.

"Then ... I will try," Laela said, "but you will have to teach me in ... case I do anything ... wrong."

The Marquis did not answer. He merely kissed her.

Then it was impossible to go on talking.

They both knew they were already united by love and even the Marriage Service could not make them any closer.

* * *

They had luncheon in the Dining-Room which made Laela speechless with admiration.

Then, just before she went upstairs, the Marquis said to her:

"I have something to tell you which I think will make you happy."

"What is it?" Laela asked.

"I have told my Secretary to send a carriage for your brother Peter and the Governess with whom he is staying and bring them here."

Laela stared at him as if she felt she could not have heard right.

The Marquis went on:

"I have a relation who lives on the Estate who has two sons of about the same age as Peter. I am going to suggest they come and stay at Eagles while you and I go away on our honeymoon."

He kissed her before he added:

"I feel the boys will enjoy riding my horses, fishing in the lake, and doing all the things I did when I was their age."

For a moment Laela was speechless.

Then the tears came into her eyes and ran down her cheeks, and the Marquis asked:

"My darling, why are you crying? What have I said to upset you?"

"They are . . . tears of . . . happiness because . . . you are so . . . kind," she sobbed. "How could any . . . man be . . . so . . . understanding and so . . . absolutely . . . unbelievably . . . wonderful?"

Then she was in his arms and the Marquis held her close.

"H-how can I . . . ever tell . . . you how . . . marvellous you are?" she asked with a little sob.

"You can tell me later," the Marquis said as he smiled, "and it is something I shall be waiting eagerly to hear."

Gently he wiped away her tears.

Then he said:

"Now go upstairs and make youself even lovelier than you are already. I want to remember for the rest of my life how my Bride looked to-day."

"I will . . . try to look . . . lovely for you," Laela said. "What . . . whatever my face . . . looks like . . . my heart is yours completely!"

"That is all I want," the Marquis answered.

He kissed her again and she ran upstairs.

In the Queen's Room Mrs. Meadows, the House-keeper, was waiting for her.

Her simple white muslin evening-gown had been ironed while she was at luncheon and she changed into it.

Mrs. Meadows placed a Brussels lace veil on her head which made her gown no longer simple, but glamorous.

There was a small tiara of diamonds made in the shape of wild flowers which the Marquis had chosen for her to wear.

She wore a matching necklace.

When she looked at herself in the mirror, Laela found it hard to know who she was.

How could she be the same girl who had been sewing diligently so that she would be able to live in a cottage?

Before she left the bed-room a footman handed in a bouquet of white orchids.

They had just come into bloom, he said, in one of the Marquis's greenhouses.

"You looks real lovely, Miss!" the Housekeeper said as Laela was ready to go downstairs. "An' you're just the lady we've all been hoping His Lordship would take as a wife."

"Thank . . . you," Laela said in her soft voice. "I only hope . . . I . . . will not . . . disappoint you."

"You'll not do that," Mrs. Meadows replied, "and I know that God'll bless you both on this happy day!"

Laela went slowly down the stairs to where the Marquis was waiting for her in the hall.

He was looking very smart with the blue Ribbon of the Garter across his chest.

There was a number of decorations on his coat—two for gallantry.

But his eyes were filled with love, and that was all that mattered.

He knew Laela was nervous, and he kissed her hand before he placed it on his arm.

As they walked slowly down the passage which led to the Chapel at the back of the house, he said softly:

"I love you, Laela, and this is the way I always wanted to be married: very quietly in my own Chapel by my own Chaplain, and be alone with the woman I love."

Laela's smile was all he needed to tell him how much what he had said meant to her.

It was spoken in all sincerity.

If he had married anybody else, he would have been forced to have a huge wedding at St. George's, Hanover Square, and perhaps a Reception at Carlton House, with all the gossips in London there, criticising his wife because she was not "one of them."

"This is the right beginning," he told himself, "for a marriage which will be different from what anyone expects."

As they knelt in the beautiful Chapel with its stained glass windows, Laela felt that her Mother and Father were present.

There were angels singing overhead.

Then, as the Vicar blessed their union, she knew she had also been blessed in a manner she had never expected, not because the Marquis was rich, but because he loved her.

He was everything she wanted a man to be.

When the ceremony was over, they went into the Drawing-Room, which she had not seen before.

The Senior Servants, like Mullins, who had been at Eagles for thirty years, and Mrs. Meadows even longer, were there.

The heads of every department toasted their health in champagne.

The Marquis made a short speech thanking them for their good wishes and for their long years of service.

He added that he hoped they would help his wife and finished by saying:

"You have made this a home for me ever since I was born. I want my wife, who has lost both her parents, to feel it is a home for her, and, of course, for our children and the generations that will come after us."

The servants cheered him.

There were tears in Mrs. Meadows's eyes and in those of the old Cook who had been at Eagles since the Marquis was a small boy.

The servants continued to drink their health, but the Marquis took Laela upstairs.

He showed her first the *Boudoir* which opened out of her bed-room on one side and his own on the other.

It was a lovely room filled with treasures that had been collected by each succeeding Marchioness of Mounteagle.

Laela had no time to look at them.

The Marquis took her into his room, where the huge four-poster bed had the coat of arms of the Mounteagles embroidered on the headboard.

There had been flowers in the *Boudoir*, but Laela saw now there were lilies which scented the air in the Marquis's room.

He shut the door and said:

"At last, my Darling, I know you are mine. Nobody can take you from me, and I can tell you how much I love you!"

Laela lifted her face to his.

He kissed her gently, as if he were still moved by the Service in which they had just taken part.

Then, as he felt the rapture and wonder of her sweep

over him, he lifted the tiara from her head.

Then he threw the Brussels lace veil down on the floor.

Her gown followed, and he lifted her onto the huge four-poster bed.

She had not spoken while he was kissing her.

It was impossible to express in words the ecstasy his kisses gave her.

Thrills ran through her body because he was touching her.

Now, as he joined her and pulled her into his arms, she turned to hide her face against his shoulder.

"My Darling! My sweet!" the Marquis said. "How can I tell you how much you mean to me! I have never known real happiness until this moment."

She moved a little closer to him.

Then she said in a very small voice:

"I . . . I have . . . something to . . . tell you."

The Marquis stiffened.

It flashed through his mind that she had a confession to make.

Perhaps it was something that she had done in the past like Fleur and every other woman he had ever known.

He felt he could not bear to be disillusioned now, at the last minute.

He had been so confident that she was different that he wanted to beg her not to tell him anything.

He would make her keep it a secret.

Then he knew if he did so he would be eternally curious, which would be even worse than knowing the truth.

"What is—it?" he asked, and there was a raw note in his voice.

There was a little pause. Then Laela said:

"I know . . . you will . . . think I am . . . very stupid . . . and perhaps it is . . . something I should . . .
not tell you . . ."

The Marquis waited.

He felt as if everything around him had gone cold.

Laela hid her face again and said in a whisper:

"I have . . . thought and . . . thought . . . but I have . . .
no idea how . . . two people like us . . . make . . .
l-love . . . I am so . . . afraid I shall . . . do something . . . which you dislike . . . and you . . . will stop . . .
loving . . . me."

The last words came brokenly from her lips.

The Marquis felt as if the whole world were filled
with sunlight.

For a moment he shut his eyes as if the relief was
almost too over-whelming.

Then he said:

"My Darling, my lovely one, my precious, innocent
little wife, do you think I want you to know anything
about love, except what I shall teach you?"

He kissed her passionately—her lips, her mouth, her
breasts.

Her body quivered against his and her breath came
in little gasps.

"I . . . love . . . you. Oh . . . I . . . love . . . you."

"You are mine—mine, Laela!" he said.

His voice deepened and became more possessive as
he went on:

"I will kill any man who touches you, and I think I
would kill you, too, if I thought you were unfaithful
to me."

"How could I . . . possibly be that," Laela asked,
"when . . . I love . . . and adore . . . you? In fact, if I

am . . . truthful, I . . . worship you. Oh . . . my wonderful . . . wonderful husband, teach me . . . how to
make . . . you happy!"

The Marquis found her lips.

Then he was kissing her fiercely, demandingly, and
possessively.

It was different from how he had ever kissed her
before, but Laela was not afraid.

Something wild and exciting leapt within her.

She felt as if there were flames in her breasts and on
her lips.

They were part of the fire burning in him.

"I . . . love . . . you! I . . . love . . . you!" she wanted to
say and go on saying.

But there was no need to say anything.

As the Marquis made her his, there was the song
of the Angels, the light of Heaven, and a glory that
radiated from God.

This was love—Spiritual and Divine.

The love that all men seek and some are privileged
to find.

Miss Cartland in 1978 sang an Album of Love Songs with the Royal Philharmonic Orchestra.

In private life Barbara Cartland, who is a Dame of the Order of St. John of Jerusalem, Chairman of the St. John Council in Hertfordshire and Deputy President of the St. John Ambulance Brigade, has fought for better conditions and salaries for Midwives and Nurses.

She championed the cause for the Elderly in 1956 invoking a Government Enquiry into the "Housing Condition of Old People."

In 1962 she had the Law of England changed so that Local Authorities had to provide camps for their own Gypsies. This has meant that since then thousands and thousands of Gypsy children have been able to go to School, which they had never been able to do in the past, as their caravans were moved every twenty-four hours by the Police.

There are now fourteen camps in Hertfordshire and Barbara Cartland has her own Romany Gypsy Camp called Barbaraville by the Gypsies.

Her designs "Decorating with Love" are being sold all over the U.S.A. and the National Home Fashions League made her, in 1981, "Woman of Achievement."

She is unique in that she was one and two in the Dalton list of Best Sellers, and one week had four books in the top twenty.

Barbara Cartland's book *Getting Older, Growing Younger* has been published in Great Britain and the U.S.A. and her fifth cookery book, *The Romance of Food*, is now being used by the House of Commons.

In 1984 she received at Kennedy Airport America's Bishop Wright Air Industry Award for her contribution to the development of aviation. In 1931 she and two R.A.F. Officers thought of, and carried, the first aeroplane-towed glider airmail.

During the War she was Chief Lady Welfare Officer in Bedfordshire, looking after 20,000 Servicemen and -women. She thought of having a pool of Wedding Dresses at the War Office so a Service Bride could hire a gown for the day.

She bought 1,000 gowns without coupons for the A.T.S., the W.A.A.F.'s and the W.R.E.N.S. In 1945 Barbara Cartland received the Certificate of Merit from Eastern Command.

In 1964 Barbara Cartland founded the National Association for Health of which she is the President, as a front for all the Health Stores and for any product made as alternative medicine.

This is now a £65 million turnover a year, with one-third going in export.

In January 1988 she received *La Médaille de Vermeil de la Ville de Paris*. This is the highest award to be given in France by the City of Paris. She has sold 25 million books in France.

In March 1988 Barbara Cartland was asked by the Indian Government to open their Health Resort outside Delhi. This is almost the largest Health Resort in the world.

Barbara Cartland was received with great enthusiasm by her fans, who feted her at a reception in the City, and she received the gift of an embossed plate from the Government.

Barbara Cartland was made a Dame of the Order of the British Empire in the 1991 New Year's Honours List by Her Majesty, The Queen, for her contribution to Literature and also for her years of work for the community.